MASAAKI TACHIHARA

Translated by Stephen W. Kohl

T0165971

WIND <small>AND</small>

STONE

A NOVEL

STONE BRIDGE PRESS

Berkeley, California

Published by STONE BRIDGE PRESS
P.O. Box 8208, Berkeley, CA 94707

Originally published in Japan as *Yume wa kareno o* by
Masaaki Tachihara in 1979.
Copyright © Mitsuyo Tachihara.
English translation copyright © 1992 by Stephen W. Kohl.
Printed in the United States of America.
Illustration on page 127 by Donald Dean.
Book design by David Bullen.

LIBRARY OF CONGRESS CATALOGING-IN-PUBLICATION DATA

Tachihara Masaaki, 1926–1980.
[Yume wa kareno o. English]
Wind and stone : a novel / Masaaki Tachihara :
translated by Stephen W. Kohl.
p. cm.
Translation of: Yume wa kareno o.
ISBN 0-9628137-7-x (pbk.)
I. Title.
PL862.A25Y8813   1992
895.6´35—dc20   92-12031
CIP

CONTENTS

ILLUSTRATIONS

STONES

(The Garden at Ryoanji)

1

It had been fourteen years since Mizue first met Yusaku Kase. It was autumn the year she turned eighteen and began commuting from Oiso northwest to college in Tokyo. Returning from school in the city to her home one evening, she found a young man working with Old Kane the gardener.

"Well, look who's here; it's the young lady of the house," Old Kane said.

The younger man wore an alpine hat. She guessed he was twenty-four or twenty-five years old. The shovel in his hands paused momentarily as he glanced at her. Then he returned to work. They were digging a hole to bury the fallen leaves.

"The boy's a college graduate," explained Old Kane, "but he says he wants to become a gardener. He's been with me about a month now. He'll probably be working for you from now on, so I want you to know he has my recommendation." Old Kane did all the talking; the young man remained silent as he leveled the ground over the buried leaves. His face had a certain tenseness that made him seem distant and unapproachable.

Early the following summer, when Old Kane came to trim the new growth, he came alone. "Didn't young Kase come with you?" Mizue's father asked. He was drinking his morning tea in the small garden adjoining his tea room. Every day before he went to work he would have his tea here, at the stone water basin that sat by the tea room's low entrance.

"He quit," replied Old Kane.

"Did he go to work for someone else?"

"I don't know. He knows his gardens, though; he'll be a hard one to replace."

"Did you quarrel or something?"

"No, nothing like that. He just up and left."

This was all Mizue knew about Yusaku Kase. She made no special effort to cherish the memory of the young man, but somehow she did remember — she remembered that autumn evening they first met, and she remembered the early summer morning when her father and Old Kane had talked about him.

Mizue graduated from college in Tokyo in spring of the year she turned twenty-two. In autumn the following year she left her parents' home and married Eiji Shida, who was four years older. A year later her son, Eiichi, was born, and a year after that she gave birth to a daughter, Noriko. In June of her twenty-ninth year her father passed away at the family home at Oiso. Having retired from his position as president of an investment bank, he had been enjoying the days spent puttering around in his garden. Within three months of her husband's death, Mizue's mother too passed away; it was as if she did not want to be left behind. Mizue's older brother was living in Tokyo, where he ran a small company, and since there was no longer anyone at the family home, the place was put up for sale. The house, built before the depression, had been standing for some forty years, so the real value of the property was in its nearly half acre of land. Her brother's business had apparently not been doing well for some time, so Mizue, supposing he needed the money, agreed to the sale. The house went quickly and Mizue, at her brother's request, lent him her share of the money. Toward the end of that year he took poison and killed himself.

Having the funerals of all three family members within a single year left Mizue desolate. But in the past four years of her marriage to Eiji, now a manager at the Shida Ham Company, her daily life was in no way unusual; yet deep within her remained the dark shadow of her loss. On some days the memory of this loss seemed unendurable.

The main offices of the Shida Ham Company were located at Fujisawa, a small city southwest of Tokyo on the busy Tokaido Train Line, while the processing plants were nearby at Atsugi and Hiratsuka. The business had been in the Shida family for three generations. The current president, Sakuzo Shida, had his home on the coast at Kugenuma near Fujisawa. His elder son, Eizo, representing the fourth generation, was expected to take over the business, so he and his wife lived in Sakuzo's house. Eiji Shida was the second son; at the time of his marriage to Mizue he was made manager of the processing plant at Atsugi. He and Mizue built a small house nearby and lived there. Atsugi had been a quiet place when they built their home, but in the intervening years the town had grown rapidly. Many people had moved in, and it had become a noisy, suburban city. So, two years ago, in the autumn, Eiji bought a parcel of land in nearby Hadano.

He had liked Hadano for a long time because of the way the Tanzawa mountains towered behind the city in a solid wall. Several streams flowed out of nearby marshland. The property Eiji bought was situated near the middle fork of one of them, the Kaneme River, on nearly a quarter acre of gently sloping land. The first thing Eiji did was ask an architect to draw up plans for a house. At two stories, built of wood and with a tile roof, it was the most imposing house in the neighborhood when it was completed the end of the previous year. As soon as he and Mizue had moved from Atsugi into their new house, Eiji said, "Next we do the garden."

In many families the elder brother and heir does not have much business sense, but in the Shida family this was not so. The elder brother, Eizo, was an aggressive businessman while Eiji, the younger brother, was more deliberate and traditional. When Eizo came to see the new house he asked,"What's all this talk about a garden? That's a waste of money. Just plant a few trees in the right places and let it go at that."

Nevertheless, Eiji Shida still wanted to build a decent Japanese garden. A friend from his school days named Kawada worked for a publishing company. One day Eiji called him and asked if he knew anyone who could build a garden for him. One Saturday afternoon shortly thereafter, Kawada came to Hadano with a landscape architect.

"Occasionally our magazine runs a photo feature on a garden built by Mr. Kase. He won't make any commitment without seeing the site first, so I brought him over," said Kawada.

Mizue was bringing tea for the guests when she heard the name Kase mentioned. Taking another look at the landscape architect, she saw it was indeed Yusaku Kase. Long ago when she had met him at the old family home at Oiso, he had appeared to be twenty-four or twenty-five—Mizue counted up the years and months that had passed; he must be almost forty by now. He did not seem as tense as he had then, but that distant, unapproachable expression remained.

I don't suppose he even remembers me, she thought.

Kase agreed to draw up plans for the garden. "A garden designer," he declared, "must not make a garden simply to suit his own taste. But if all he does is what his client tells him to do, the garden will have an oddly vulgar air about it. Once I finish the plans, I'd like to have you look at them."

Kase took the blueprints and left.

When he had gone, Shida asked Kawada, "What sort of person is he?"

"He won't build a garden unless the client can afford a traditional wooden house with a tile roof. He feels that when a house is made of reinforced concrete, or when it is prefabricated, the effect of the garden is ruined. The appearance of the house is ruined too, so he won't have anything to do with it. He's the eldest son in a family that operates a wholesale fish cake business in Odawara. He studied economics at school, but turned the family business over to his brother and devoted himself completely to the art of garden building. He's been married twice. Each time his wife walked out on him. When he's building a garden for someone far away, he stays at the client's house for months on end and never goes home. Apparently his wives just lost patience and left him. The interesting thing is that both times, after they had been away for several months, the wives wanted to come back to him. But he seems utterly unattached to worldly things, and he wouldn't take either of them back again."

"That is interesting, isn't it?"

Overhearing this story about Kase's life, Mizue supposed that the women who had walked out on him had really done so out of despair at having been abandoned. When Kase was talking about the garden, Mizue realized that there was something about him that attracted women and never released them. Indeed, she now recalled vividly the late autumn day fourteen years ago when she had first met him. She had not intended it, but that brief glimpse had remained in her memory, and the image was clarified today by seeing Kase in the flesh. Perhaps this was because now she could look at him with the eyes of a mature woman; she had been too young before.

2

By the end of March all the plans had been drawn and Kase was ready to begin work on the front garden. Mizue learned from her husband that the job would take about two months.

On the first day Kase showed up at nine o'clock with three young gardeners who were his assistants. Kase was dressed as a gardener, but the assistants looked more like university students.

"I'll be back around noon. See you then," Shida told Kase as he drove off to the plant at Atsugi.

Mizue left the kitchen work to her maid, Momoko, and began sweeping and dusting the living room. As she worked, she looked out the sliding glass doors to watch Kase giving instructions to his three young helpers. Soon they were unloading large stones for the garden from two medium-sized trucks. One truck had a crane mounted on it to unload the larger stones.

When she finished cleaning the living room, Mizue told Momoko to take tea out to them at ten o'clock. Then she set out to do some shopping. She had not prepared any snacks to go with their afternoon tea at three o'clock, so she intended to find something suitable at the market. Hadano was in a rural area with few good shops, but there was one shop that made and sold rice cakes. Mizue decided they would do if she toasted them with soy sauce and wrapped them in seaweed.

By the time she finished shopping and returned home, all the stones for the garden had been unloaded. Kase and his assistants were drinking tea on the veranda with the plans and sketches spread out before them. All the stones, large and small alike, were black, and some had moss growing on them.

Shortly after noon Shida returned home. By that time the arrangement of the stones and the way each was to be set into the ground had been decided. The house had about 3,200 square feet of floor space, with 2,000 square feet on the ground floor and 1,200 on the second. Some 9,000 square feet of land remained for the garden, and of this approximately 7,000 would be used for the front and middle gardens. A dozen or more trees were already growing along both the south and east sides of the house, and these natural areas would actually become part of the overall garden design.

Over lunch Mizue commented to her husband, "He's certainly using a dark stone."

"It's called Fuji stone. They used more colorful stones in the garden for that new house just at the foot of the mountain. They're kind of greenish, but we won't be using any stones like that here."

"What about under the eaves? If we don't hurry and put in concrete or some sort of stones, we'll be flooded when it rains."

"For the drip line there'll be a white granite called Isegoro. It's made into round stones, about the size of my fist. Kase will set those in around the eaves. Anyway, I'm looking forward to having the garden completed."

Just then Kase and his three assistants returned from Hadano, where they had gone for lunch. Shida took a quick swallow of tea and went out into the garden. Mizue watched Kase walk over to Shida and then overheard them talking.

"We can finish getting all the stones placed today," said Kase, "but I expect it will be about half a month before we can set the granite along the drip line. In the meantime, there are several nurseries at Miyahara in Fujisawa, and someday when you have time we ought to go take a look at their trees."

"I can go any time," replied Shida.

"How about now?"

"That's fine with me. It takes only half an hour to get to Miyahara from here."

Kase gave instructions to his assistants and got into Shida's car. The two men drove off.

At three o'clock Mizue took tea out to the assistants. "Are you apprenticed to Mr. Kase?" she asked.

The young men looked at each other, puzzled. Finally one replied, "Everyone in our school's landscape architecture department is learning gardening from Mr. Kase."

"Oh, really! You mean Mr. Kase teaches at a university?"

"He's an instructor, but he rarely shows up at school. Instead he leaves messages saying where he's working on a garden so we can come and get actual experience."

The existing trees in the garden were oak, maple, and Japanese snowbell, and the gardeners placed a number of the large, black Fuji stones among them. As Mizue watched from the window, a large stone, perhaps six feet high, was dropped into a hole in the ground; less than half of it was left visible.

Wouldn't it do just as well, thought Mizue, to use a stone half that size? But perhaps that's not the way gardens are made.

It was after four o'clock when Shida and Kase returned. "I'll leave it up to you where the trees we get should be placed," said Shida as they sat on the veranda drinking tea. "I have to get back to work for a while."

At five o'clock Kase and his crew stopped work and went home. Mizue had no notion how the garden was going to turn out. Even when she looked at the plans and drawings, she had no idea what they meant. She did know, however, that she felt a vague disquiet. She tried to think it out, to decide what sort of uneasiness she felt and why it should well up within her this way, but she could find no explanation for it.

3

By the end of May, the stones were set, the trees planted, and the lawn installed. The front garden was nearly complete. This did not mean, however, that Kase and his crew had come to work every day. They did not work on rainy days, of course, and there were days when only the three assistants, or sometimes only two of them, showed up.

As the garden began to reveal its form to her, Mizue felt she was glimpsing the shape of this man Kase as well. The completed garden did not give the impression of artifice. The existing trees had been so carefully used that the natural mountain slope seemed a part of the garden. A streamlike configuration of small stones was set among the trees, and when it rained the water would follow this bed down the slope to the Kaneme River. Especially impressive was Kase's foresight in using subtle, dark stones. Rather than creating a garden that called attention to its remarkable stones, here the stones sat in quiet harmony with the trees.

"This is exactly right! What a garden!" Shida exclaimed.

Kase said he wanted to wait until autumn to build the middle garden, which was to be in the dry landscape style, with nothing but stones and gravel and moss. During the summer rainy season he would try growing some bamboo, and if it took root he would make it into a bamboo grove linking the middle and back gardens. The back garden would then be designed to fit in with the bamboo, while between the bamboo and the middle garden he would build a low earthen wall.

"Please do not grow any other shrubs or plants in this garden. Western flowers particularly would be out of place here. Two years ago I built a garden in Kamakura for a family that had just made a lot of money in real estate. The house was all right and the construction of the garden was fine. I spent three months working on it. When I went back to see it again six months later, I found that someone from Chichibu had come along selling cheap stones and that they had bought lots of large colored ones and placed them here and there in the garden. There was nothing I could do about it, but it made me very angry. So, I'll ask you to wait for three years; then if you don't like the garden any more, or if you feel it isn't interesting, I won't mind if you build a completely new one." Kase said this the day the front garden was completed. "For me," he then said quietly, "building a garden is a struggle against mediocrity."

Overhearing Kase's words, Mizue understood that this man would not come to the house again until autumn, and she felt she would be released from the uneasiness that had been with her the past two months. Yet somehow she felt no relief. For two months she had been trying to come to grips with her discomfort, but still she did not understand it. Was it an uncertainty she had about herself? Fourteen years ago she had failed to see in Kase the man that she as a woman should have seen, but that was no reason Kase should make her uneasy now. From that day fourteen years ago the flow of time had swept her along in tranquillity.

Eiji Shida was a man of refined taste. He read literature, appreciated music, and even had some understanding of painting. He felt he appreciated the arts even though he himself was not an artist. For a man of such refinement, a ham processing business seemed a trivial waste of time.

Mizue was satisfied with such a husband; they had been married now for eleven years. As husband and wife they soon learned that their needs as man and woman were different, but they still managed to bring their two lives together. Mizue had first become truly aware of herself as a woman in the summer of her twenty-seventh year, a year after her second child was born. It seemed strange to her. Pursue it as she would, whatever she was looking for always eluded her. And though she sensed that along the way she might well confront death, she nevertheless threw herself into the pursuit. It was at this time too that she experienced a feeling of disquiet. As she gradually resumed her sexual life, this uncertainty disappeared.

Mizue's father had died on the twenty-fourth of June four years ago. Being the second son in his family, he had lived separately from the main family in Tokyo. He had requested that he be buried at the temple at his home of Oiso. The previous June Mizue and Shida had observed the third anniversary of his passing. Since Mizue's mother and brother died the same year, all three third-year observances had been held simultaneously. This year Mizue had visited the graves during the spring equinox and prayed for the happiness of all three souls.

June twenty-fourth was a cloudy day. At breakfast Mizue told her husband that she planned to visit the cemetery at Oiso that afternoon.

"Oh, really? Today is the anniversary of your father's death? Then by all means go."

"It would be nice if I could stop on the way at Kugenuma to see your parents, but I won't have time today. I'll drop by next time."

"I'm sure that will be all right. After all, you get to Kugenuma one way or another several times a year."

When her husband had finished breakfast, he left for the plant at Atsugi. Mizue took care of a few small chores during the morning and set out shortly before noon. It was too early in the season to wear linen clothing, but the weather was muggy, so she wore a silk summer kimono.

In front of Hadano Station she boarded a bus that followed the Kaneme River downstream to the coastal town of Hiratsuka, and from there she could get either a train or a bus to Oiso. At Hiratsuka she consulted the train schedule at the station and found a through train for Numazu leaving in seven minutes. Mizue bought a ticket and went onto the platform.

Getting off the train at Oiso, just a stop or two away, she walked along the platform and was about to ascend the stairs to the exit when she heard a voice. She turned around, wondering if someone was calling her, and there was Kase, wearing mourning clothes and a black necktie.

"Oh, Mr. Kase." Mizue was flustered at this unexpected meeting.

"Kane died yesterday, and the funeral is being held today. The old man was very helpful to me in many ways, so I came today to pay my last respects."

"You mean Old Kane the gardener?"

"That's right, the one who worked for your father."

"Oh, then you did remember me."

"Yes, of course I remembered. Kane told me once that you had married a meat dealer. Your husband has a ham company, doesn't he?"

"That first time we met was so long ago I supposed you had forgotten who I was, so I didn't say anything about it. Today happens to be the anniversary of my father's death, so I'm on my way to visit the temple."

"I see."

Kase started up the stairs ahead of her.

"Old Kane must have been very old."

"I expect he was seventy-five or -six."

They reached the top of the stairs and took another flight down the other side of the overpass before they exited through the ticket taker's gate.

"Is your father's temple near here?"

"Yes, it's only about a ten-minute walk."

"How would you like to have lunch together later?"

"Why yes, I would like that, but can you afford the time?"

"Sure. I'll wait for you at the eel restaurant. It's been a long time since I had a chance to eat Oiso eels. Well, see you later, then."

Kase took the road that sloped off to the left. Mizue walked along the road to the right that followed the railroad tracks. She stopped at a florist's shop to buy flowers for the graves. Kase had simply said "the eel restaurant" at Oiso, but there was only one such place that was well known. Mizue had often ordered food from there when she was living in the town.

After visiting the graves, Mizue made an offering at the temple and left. Forty minutes after leaving Kase, she reached the eel restaurant.

"Has Mr. Kase arrived yet?" she asked the young woman sitting behind the counter.

"Yes, I believe he is upstairs."

A large room on the second floor had several low tables in it. Two other groups of guests were eating. Kase sat alone, drinking beer.

"I certainly didn't expect to run into you today." Mizue took her seat across the table from Kase.

"Will you join me?" he asked, indicating the beer bottle.

"Yes, I'll have a glass."

"You must have had a very difficult time a few years back. I didn't know until Kane told me, much later, that all your family had died."

"Yes. It was a very difficult year."

"It always seems so unexpected when someone dies. Last year I was building a garden for a man in Fukushima. It took from spring right through autumn. He was a man of some refinement, in his forties, just in the prime of life. We planned to get together for a few drinks this spring, so I went to see him as I had promised, but as usual without bothering to phone. Well, I found out he had suffered a heart attack in February and was dead. I had another experience that was even worse; once a friend and I had been out drinking together and a few hours later he was dead. For several years now I've had the idea that death is something that always comes when you least expect it. I will be forty next year and soon I expect I will have to begin thinking about my own death."

"Are you that old?"

"I suppose I will have a few gardens to leave behind when I die. And a book on building gardens will be finished before long. One book and a few gardens; that should be enough. Your husband, you know, has a good understanding of the garden I'm building at your house, and the natural contours of the land are nice. I think it will turn out quite well. In three years it should be mature enough to have sabi, to have that weathered quality of beauty."

Listening to Kase talk, Mizue felt an odd sensation. It reminded her of wind blowing among the stones on a barren mountain slope. He's a strange man, she thought, now uneasy. This was the same feeling she'd had when Kase began working on the garden.

When Mizue and Kase finished eating and left the eel shop, the clouds had cleared away and the street was bathed in pale sunlight.

"Your home is down in Odawara, isn't it?"

"I only go back to Odawara once in a while, to eat the fish cakes my family makes. I live up in Yokohama, but I'm away when I'm doing a job out of town."

Shida had received a business card from Kase with only the address of his Tokyo office printed on it, so all Mizue could remember was that Kase's family lived some place in Odawara, a bit farther down the coast to the west.

The two arrived at Oiso Station ten minutes before their train came. While waiting they sat together on a bench in the middle of the platform. Neither spoke.

When Mizue got off at Hiratsuka, she thanked Kase for the meal, but he only nodded politely and said, "Oh, it was nothing."

When Shida returned home that evening, Mizue told him about running into Kase at Oiso that afternoon, but she left out the part about their meal together. She was not sure why she felt guilty, and that disturbed her. She had done nothing wrong, of course, and she might just as well have mentioned going to the restaurant. Still, she left it out. Later she felt badly about omitting it, but by then she could hardly go back and add it on.

"So, Old Kane died, did he? I met him several times at the house at Oiso."

Shida did not seem concerned that she had met Kase.

4

Shida asked one of the local gardeners from Hadano, a young man named Ume, to handle the matter of transplanting the bamboo into the back garden during the rainy season. They would have to wait until autumn to know whether or not the bamboo would take root. After putting in the bamboo, Ume got twenty bales of decayed leaves from Tanzawa to spread around the roots. This not only served as fertilizer, but also protected the plants.

"I expect they will grow now," he said. It had been arranged that Ume would also take care of the garden after it was built.

The rainy season passed and the clear sky of summer was upon them. One afternoon Mizue went to town to do shopping, and as she passed the open plaza in front of the train station she noticed it was filled with hikers carrying their backpacks. Hadano was busy this time of year with crowds of young people who came to climb Mount Tanzawa.

On another such afternoon, Kase called. He asked how the bamboo was doing and if it had taken root.

"I have no idea how it is doing, but it seems to be all right." It seemed years since she had heard his voice.

"When your husband comes home, will you tell him I would like to come by tomorrow morning. If possible I want to have the middle garden finished by mid-August." Kase stated his business and hung up.

Kase showed up the next morning at nine o'clock with two of the student gardeners who had been with him before. He went around the back garden with a shovel, digging holes here and there to see how the bamboo roots were doing. As he worked, he talked to his two assistants.

After a time Kase returned to the front garden and announced that the roots were in good shape. "I have to be in Kyoto this autumn for an extended stay, so if it's all right with you, I would like to get to work on this project right away tomorrow morning."

"That's fine with me. The sooner the better as far as I'm concerned," replied Shida, looking over his shoulder at the middle garden. It had just been weeded a few days earlier. The middle garden extended as far as the north side of the tea room, which was also used as a spare guest room. Kase's plan had the bamboo grove along the north side of the room, separated from the garden on the east side by an earthen wall. The north side would then become a dry landscape—or *karesansui*—garden, and the south side would be a tea garden. When visitors came to the Shida home, they would normally pass along a corridor from the entryway to reach the guest room, but if a guest was especially discerning in these matters, he could instead be shown by way of the front garden directly into the tea garden. The tea room itself had a portable hearth in the summer and autumn, and a regular hearth to heat the tea water during the winter and spring months. Shida found a small tea room disagreeable and had had his built to nearly twice the normal size. He had also had the area used to store tea equipment made of plain wood rather than straw mats. An adjoining room was furnished Western style, but Shida showed it only to his close friends.

Work on the garden began the following morning.

First Kase and his crew excavated the middle garden to a depth of about fifteen inches. Then they set the black stones upright and just a bit to the east when viewed from the tea room. Smaller stones, not quite perpendicular, were placed to the left and behind these large stones. Next the men dug a trench three feet deep and filled it with cement; this was to be the foundation for the earthen wall, but Kase said it would also prevent the bamboo roots from spreading to the south. While this was work that any common laborer could do, Kase did the job with his own hands.

"Once this foundation is set, the bamboo roots will be forced to spread east and west," he explained to his young helpers.

Mizue watched the work progress up to this point and then set about her housework. She brought tea to the gardeners at three o'clock. As she placed a cup in front of Kase she was aware of her strong feeling of disquiet. She could smell the earth and sweat on Kase's body even from a distance.

I always seem to feel uneasy when he's around, she thought. Nothing's happened between us, but he makes me self-conscious and restless.

Mizue was reminded again of that awful year she lost all three members of her family. Her gloominess then had had nothing to do with her husband and children. There were odd times when she felt her gloom would never end, that all she could do was immerse herself in it. Now, Mizue was again having these old feelings.

"I hope you enjoy your tea." Mizue set out some cakes for the men and returned to the house. Her restiveness was very real indeed. Still, she could find no definite source for it. It did not occur to her that Kase could be the source; she did not know him well enough. She was able to continue believing in her own innocence, even in his presence.

It took sixteen days to finish the dry landscape garden. It was designed so that when the garden was viewed from the tea room, the wall of the house formed its western side while the low earthen walls bounded it on the north and east. Just beyond the north wall was the bamboo grove. Within the garden walls, white sand raked into wavelike patterns surrounded the outside tea room, and in the background rose the perpendicular black stones. A bed of moss encircled the two stones in the center. A smaller stone in the northeast corner by the wall was also bordered by moss. A band of earth had been added up to the white sand so the patch of moss could grow and expand.

On the evening of the day this middle garden was completed, Shida asked Kase into the house for a few drinks and to thank him for his work. "The front garden and the middle garden are nicely balanced," said Shida. "But tell me, since you studied economics at school, how did you become interested in building gardens?"

"I guess there was no real reason for it," said Kase. "If I really had to, I would say it's the influence of Japanese Buddhism. The Pure Land and Shinshu sects both believe in salvation by grace, while the Shingon, Tendai, and Zen sects teach that one must save himself through his own efforts. I suppose I've been influenced by Zen, and my effort at salvation is building gardens."

In the end Kase would not say much more about his work; he only engaged in the usual idle chatter people exchange over drinks. It was hard to say whether he was self-conscious about discussing his own work, or whether he found the questions of laymen annoying.

Kase's drinking was restrained and formal. Mizue realized that her uneasiness was gone now that the middle garden was completed and Kase would no longer be coming to the house. She felt the same way she had at the end of May when the front garden was finished. But she found no relief this time either. Still, after tomorrow everything would fall back into its normal, uneventful pattern. Mizue had confidence in herself as a wife.

From that day, summer quickly drew to an end.

5

The garden Kase built began to change and slowly reveal itself just about the time in October when the trees were losing their leaves. Mizue surveyed the garden every day when she got up; each morning, it seemed to have changed its aspect during the night.

The shrubs that formed the hedge overlapped and grew together in a mixture of winter camellia, sasanqua, holly, and Japanese snowbell. The day Kase completed the garden he had instructed Ume, the young local gardener, how to care for it, and had cautioned him not to trim the hedge too evenly.

"Only use the shears where you have to. It won't do if the hedge is too much like a barrier. When we glimpse the view beyond the hedge, we are looking into the outside world, the world of other people. So I never want the hedge to look like it's been freshly clipped. In the *Pillow Book of Sei Shonagon* there is a scene where 'Three or four crows fly off, two or three more follow.' You see what I mean? I want no clear distinction between the garden, the hedge, and the world beyond. In winter, this hedge will be the most prominent feature of the garden."

Just as Kase had predicted, as the leaves began to fall from the trees the hedge stood out prominently. In September Ume had clipped the hedge and done his best to follow Kase's instructions, but perhaps because he had fussed over it, the hedge looked obviously trimmed.

Shida said it would probably be all right by spring when the new growth appeared.

Walking through the garden in summer, Mizue had felt the stones were alive. By early November, when the leaves had completely fallen, the stones were visible from the house. From the family room, the living room, and the tea room, she could see the stones, stones that seemed to be living things. The garden may have appeared natural and uncontrived, but in fact its design was quite geometrical.

One afternoon toward the end of November a strong wind blew through the grove of trees. The barren branches waved, and even the leaves of the hedge turned their undersides to the wind, but the stones stood still, unmoved. Each perfectly placed stone seemed to be gazing at the house with eyes that were alive. Eyes like Kase's eyes.

All through the spring and summer Kase worked in silence and did not even glance at me, Mizue thought. But what has he done? That autumn, in the garden of my parents' home, he didn't show the slightest interest in me. But he says he did notice me after all. Now these stones are where they can watch me all the time.

Only a portion of the garden right in front of the living room was covered with lawn. From here the land sloped away from the house to the grove, where dead leaves now covered the stepping stones and littered the ground between the trees. The stones here were laid out in the same pattern as those in front of the tea room. Each step was made up of three or five small stones. The stepping stones that formed the path were laid out in clusters; some were formed with a grouping of two large stones and one small one, while others were made up of five stones composed of four large ones clustered around a smaller stone. Kase had adopted a traditional pattern of stepping stones from the tea garden, and since this pattern was unusually small he had enlarged it where the path led through the grove. To Mizue, who was quite familiar with famous tea gardens, Kase's bold alteration of the form was a defiance of convention.

Some of the carefully placed stones already had moss on them, due perhaps to the moist air coming up from the river nearby.

As the days passed, the garden took on a sere but mellow aspect. Wild pheasants often appeared. Only the dry landscape of the middle garden did not change like some living creature. Pine needles were spread over the moss there to protect it from frost. But this made it seem all the more as if something alive was lurking below.

At the eel restaurant in Oiso Kase had said this garden would turn out well because of the natural contours of the land, but until now Mizue had not paid this statement any mind. Now, in the presence of this garden that exposed its wide and empty spaces to her, Mizue was again haunted by an uneasiness. She tried to see the bare trees and the evergreen hedge as nothing more than a pattern of colors and shapes. She tried to do the same with the stones. Again she had the fleeting feeling that the stones were Kase's eyes watching her. But when she looked closely at them they were just stones. Seen as part of the total garden they were flat and one-dimensional. Still, Mizue could not help feeling they were composed of invisible colors and empty spaces. She did not know what to make of this feeling. What was this invisible color? The garden's aspect in the morning was different from that in the evening. Mizue, who gazed out at the garden from the house day after day, found no relief in it.

At dawn one morning when Mizue went to the bathroom, she opened the window for ventilation. She glanced out and saw a stone she had never noticed before. She slid the window all the way open to get a better look at the black stone, which crouched at the foot of a maple tree. There could be no doubt about it: the stone was staring at her. Had there always been a stone in that place? It was only twelve feet from the bathroom. Puzzled, Mizue closed the window.

Returning to the bedroom, she looked at her own bed for a moment, took a deep breath, and slid silently into her husband's bed. He roused up and asked drowsily, "What's the matter?" They had spent the night making love and he had not expected her to come to his bed again in the morning.

"I saw something that frightened me." Mizue pressed herself against her husband's back and held her breath.

Presently he rolled over to face her, reaching for her breasts. "Did you have a dream?" he asked. Mizue kept her eyes tightly closed and did not reply. Only when her husband's hands moved lower to her thighs did she relax and yield her body to him. Even with her eyes closed she could see that stone. But the stone was not the source of her uneasiness. Sooner or later she would have to come to terms with Kase. Mizue turned this thought over vaguely in her mind, but she was brought back to reality as her husband took possession of her body.

6

When they lived in Atsugi, Mizue and Shida often had to put up with the cold wind. But in Hadano, because of the Tanzawa massif to the north, the temperature during the day was not much different from what it had been at Oiso on the coast. Nevertheless, the chill was severe at dawn and at dusk.

Early in December the sasanqua hedge began to bloom. The young gardener Ume said that sometimes it would begin blooming as early as October, but it was late this year because it had just been transplanted.

One afternoon Shida's brother, Eizo, came to the processing plant in Atsugi and then on up to the house for a visit. "I didn't realize you had such taste," said Eizo to his brother after a cursory look around the garden.

"I don't think it's too bad, as gardens go," said Eiji.

"Yes, very nice. You must have a good gardener."

"No mere gardener could make a garden like this. I hired a well-known landscape architect."

"I'm not surprised. Everything here is in the best of taste. What's his name?"

"Yusaku Kase."

"I've never heard of him. But then I don't know much about that sort of thing."

After that the brothers talked about buying pork. As she prepared tea for them, it occurred to Mizue that it really was absurd that these men who made their living buying hogs and processing ham thought they could really appreciate the design of the garden. As far as Mizue could tell, the garden at Eizo's house in Kugenuma was not very good. Every time she went there, the trees looked as if they had just been pruned. The stones' colors were garish, and the pond was filled with carp. A lot of money had been spent on the garden, that was obvious. She had heard that the carp in the pond cost as much as four thousand dollars apiece. Her husband called it typical of the *nouveau riche* style.

Eiji Shida, in contrast to his brother, was a man of refined taste. Mizue was always impressed, for example, by the fastidious care with which he would select even a summer kimono. Three years ago, on a Sunday in late spring, they had gone to Eizo's home at Kugenuma for a family get-together. A fabric dealer who occasionally came from Tokyo was there and had spread summer fabrics all around the tatami room. There were several linens: one had a white tortoise-shell pattern on a black background; another had a black tortoise-shell pattern on a white background; one was pure white; and another had an elegantly restrained off-white design. This off-white fabric epitomized the grace of *shibumi*, a quality that could be compared to the spare yet bitter flavor of the second cup of tea at a formal tea ceremony. Everyone chose the pure white linen, saying it would be coolest to wear in summer, but Eiji alone selected the elegant, off-white cloth. Mizue's father had once said it took three generations to produce a person who could appreciate a good kimono and fine food. It seemed that Eiji had inherited his grandfather's refinement.

Toward the middle of December the winter camellias began to bloom. From the house one could see flecks of red in the hedge.

"It's not good to have the winter camellias bloom too intensely. Pinch off two-thirds of the buds. That way, when they bloom in winter, the hedge has only patches of red." Mizue recalled Kase's instructions to Ume, and thought they reflected his good taste. During the autumn Ume had painstakingly pinched off the buds, and he had apparently done a good job of it.

"A really expensive garden always looks like it didn't cost much. This is that sort of garden," said Ume when he came late in the year to work.

"Have you seen a garden as fine as this anywhere else?" asked Shida.

"I've never seen one like it. None of the others is this sophisticated." Ume's reply satisfied Shida.

For Mizue, the garden accurately marked the changing seasons, and she never grew tired of it. Each day it looked different. Winter camellias do not last very long, and when it seemed the red had disappeared from one place in the hedge, blossoms would appear in another location the following morning. Seen up close, the camellias formed a red background for the stones, and the changing red patches of the blossoms altered the look of the stones as well, although the stones themselves never really changed.

The severity of the dry landscape design did not dominate this garden, yet it would suddenly make itself felt when you were not expecting it. Ordinarily a dry landscape garden is observed, but this garden looked back at you. The stone Mizue had discovered that morning at dawn from the bathroom window was one indication of this. Her husband found pleasure in looking at the garden. But one day she had the disturbing feeling that the garden had seen her naked, and had violated her.

7

Stones provided points of emphasis in a garden and its broad panorama. The flat background would be punctuated in several places; those points, however, were intended to blend into the background and to harmonize with it, giving the impression of boundlessness.

Yusaku Kase had always adhered to this principle when using stones in a dry landscape or even a conventional garden. There are several old manuals on garden design—such as *Senzui Narabini Yagyo no Zu* ("Illustrations for Designing Mountain, Water, and Hillside Field Landscapes") and *Sakuteiki* ("Treatise on Garden Making")—that every gardener should read at least once. Kase, of course, had found both these books quite useful. Another book from the eighteenth century is *Miyako Rinsen Meisho Zue*, or "Illustrations of the Capital's Famous Natural Gardens," by Akisato Rito, and contains drawings of the gardens of Kyoto temples. According to these drawings, some of the gardens remain today just as they were in the past, while others have changed slightly. At the Kyoto temple garden of Jishoji, for example, also called the Silver Pavilion, there is a mound of sand which today is shaped like an inverted bowl. But according to the old drawings, its top had at one time been broader and the mound could not have been described as bowl-shaped; it was more like a mortar. From these drawings Kase had learned how gardens did or did not change with the times. The sculptured trees at the Konchi-in garden at Nanzenji temple in Kyoto are today virtually no different now from how they were ages ago. The famous stone garden at the Ryoanji temple is similarly unchanged.

Kase was writing a book of his own on garden building because he had examined the works of his predecessors and was not satisfied by them. The publishing company where his friend Kawada worked had agreed to publish the book.

Kase's modern apartment in Yokohama hardly seemed appropriate for a landscape architect. It was located on the side of a hill about ten minutes' walk from Hodogaya Station, just southwest of downtown. His first wife, Emiko, had left him nine years earlier saying she could not put up with him any longer. His second wife, Kazue, had said the same thing when she left him four years ago. Emiko had been with him for two years, and Kazue for a year, but neither of them had had the patience to tolerate a man who was away from home more than half the time. Later, when people suggested he remarry, Kase refused, saying marriage was a nuisance. This did not mean, of course, that he did not have relations with women. He was only thirty-nine years old. Emiko had remarried, but still came to see him occasionally. She now had two children, and the youngest was old enough to go to kindergarten. Kase did not know how Emiko felt about him, and did not bother to ask. When she visited him, she was just another woman.

Up to this point in his career, Kase had built some fifty gardens. He had done both dry landscape gardens and plant and water gardens, and some of his gardens combined both styles. Whenever he designed a garden, he carefully calculated the effect time would have upon it. The process of aging in a thing of beauty is a far more important consideration in garden building than in some other arts. In the case of pottery, once a piece comes out of the kiln, its worth as a work of art can be determined, but in the case of a garden, after the builder finishes his job, nature takes over and does much of the work. An abstract garden like the stone garden at the Ryoanji temple in Kyoto was not much affected by the passage of time, but other gardens, like the one Kase built for the Shidas, needed time to mature. Since the Shidas' garden was located near a river at the foot of the mountains, Kase was counting on the moist Hadano air to bring the stones he had erected to their full potential. After some years had passed, the stones would look like they had been there for a very long time. This sort of effect was fully calculated in the garden design.

From his apartment window Kase could look down on the streets of his neighborhood of Hodogaya. From the sixth floor he could see out over the town, even to the area around the western entrance of Yokohama Station, which had become choked with office buildings in recent years. All the buildings were dyed bright red by the evening sun. Kase looked at the clock on his desk; it was shortly before five.

What shall I do? he wondered. Go out? Some days, when he had the time, he would go to Chinatown for dinner. Other days he would just go to a small restaurant nearby. He rarely cooked for himself. He had closed his office in Shibuya up in Tokyo on the twenty-fifth of December and would not reopen it until the tenth of January. He sometimes spent New Year's at his family's home in Odawara, but for the past several years he had spent the holiday at a hotel in Tokyo or Yokohama. All the stores and restaurants were closed during the first three days of the new year, and he could not remain in his apartment without food.

Nearby were an eel restaurant, a sushi bar, and a noodle stand.

I guess I'll go to Chinatown and have a look around, thought Kase, getting up from his desk. He had reserved a room at a hotel near Yokohama Station for the holiday season.

Kase got ready to go out and took the elevator down. He kept two vehicles in the apartment building parking lot but neither was a passenger car; they were medium-sized trucks he used in his work. Sometimes when he went out to eat he would drive one of the trucks, but on a night like this, when he would be drinking, he used public transportation.

As he walked toward Hodogaya Station Kase thought of Mizue. She has improved with time, just like a garden. He had been surprised to meet her again when he went to Shida's house. He could still remember the first time he had seen her fourteen years ago. He could envision clearly the slow process by which she had become a mature woman. He enjoyed thinking back about how his feelings for her had grown as he built the garden.

Kase had designed the Shidas' garden in a style he had not used recently. Building gardens is the art of copying and re-creating nature, but in the Shidas' garden Kase had used a grove of trees as an extension of the site's existing wild nature. Through the placing of the stones, he could transfer his own feelings to the garden. The garden would succeed if he could somehow symbolize nature in the arrangement of those stones. Could these stones arouse Mizue's emotions? The question had nothing to do with social values or morality, but involved his aesthetic power as a gardener. And Mizue was the object of this exercise.

Chinatown was bright and lively in anticipation of the coming holidays. Feeling a bit lonely, Kase plunged into the bustle and excitement.

TREES

(The Garden at Jishoji, "The Silver Pavilion")

1

December twenty-sixth was the last full day of work at the Atsugi and Hiratsuka processing plants of the Shida Ham Company. After the last shipment of meat was sent out on the twenty-seventh, all workers would have a holiday until January fourth.

On the twenty-eighth Shida called Ume and asked him to do some final clean-up work on the garden. Since Ume came once a month to work on the garden, there was not much to be done, just sweeping the fallen leaves and putting up the traditional New Year's pine decorations on the front gate. It was shortly after two o'clock when Ume finished the work and went home.

Since noon a charcoal fire had been kept burning in the hearth in the tea room. After Ume left, Shida made tea.

When Mizue came in to add charcoal to the fire, Shida asked, "Now that we have the house and garden all completed, wouldn't you like to have another baby?"

"Come now, at my age." Mizue blushed.

"Don't you feel lonely with only two children?"

"I'm already thirty-two. I'm too old for that."

"That's not too old to have a baby."

"But at this age it would be very disagreeable to get all swollen up. Besides, it's not the same as having a baby when you are young. If I had a baby now, I'd age very quickly."

"Yes, I suppose that's so. I guess we'll just have to get along with the two we have."

Shida was not going to insist on having a third child. He was just thinking it would be nice to have another one now that they had such a spacious house. His father frequently told him he should have more children. His brother, Eizo, had five.

When her husband asked if she would like to have another child, Mizue had looked away, saying she was too old. After Kase had completed the dry landscape, in the middle garden, he did not come to their house again. The garden he had created retained some of his vitality, but it was not the same as having him there in person. The trees in the garden had lost their leaves and their bare branches swept the wintry sky. The stones that had been concealed were now prominent. The shapes of these stones brought back memories of Kase and his odor of sweat and earth from working on the garden. Mizue had definitely been disturbed by her uneasy response to that smell. She had been vaguely uneasy too the year her brother, father, and mother had died. But then the cause was different. Now the source of her restiveness was clearly Kase. Yet she felt she did not know Kase well enough for him to cause this, and while she believed in the innocence of her own feelings toward him, it was also true that, as the days passed, she became increasingly aware of the Kase she had first met fourteen years ago. Until now Mizue had ignored the fact that Kase had also remembered her as she had been when she was eighteen; he had made that clear the day she ran into him on her way to visit the graves at Oiso. When she thought about it now, she knew she had concealed that meeting from her husband because she felt guilty that she had been unconsciously drawn to Kase.

The new year arrived. It occurred to Mizue that according to the traditional reckoning she was now another year older. A woman's thoughts and memories become deeper with the passing of the years, and so it was with Mizue's view of her own physical being. For some time now Mizue had known that she was constantly on guard against her own physical impulses. This may have been because her husband confined his physical desire to her and she had everything to gain by becoming more sensual. Although she had felt this way for some time, the coming of the new year and the addition of another year to her age brought a new ingredient to her feelings.

Mizue looked back over the past few years. They had been tranquil and satisfying, but somehow she had an odd feeling about them. There had been nothing during those years to give her life a real sense of direction. She had never felt any passionate yearning, but the past few years had seemed especially uneventful to her.

It was customary for the senior employees in the Hiratsuka and Atsugi plants to come to the Shidas' house on the third of January to express their New Year's greetings. Mizue had been busy all day getting ready for them. On the second, the family had had its own New Year's get-together at the main house in Kugenuma, but for several years now her husband, Eiji, had not put in an appearance, saying there was too much holiday traffic on the roads. To make up for it, he would take the whole family for a visit sometime after the tenth of the month.

Eiji's father, Sakuzo Shida, was president of the company, and his older brother, Eizo, was vice-president. The two men spent much of their time at the main office in Fujisawa. Eiji, a manager, spent virtually all his time at the two processing plants in Atsugi and Hiratsuka. Shida Ham was a family business, but the foremen of the plants at Atsugi and Hiratsuka were both outsiders, genial men in their fifties who had graduated from veterinary school before the war.

"On the second you go to Kugenuma, and on the third you come here. Both of you are exhausted, so next year let's not have a New Year's party here, don't you agree?" Mizue overheard her husband saying this to his two managers, and, taking his words at face value, was struck by his thoughtfulness. But even if the managers felt it was a good idea, the senior employees in the processing plants would come in any case and would not know what to do if they could not go somewhere to offer their New Year's greetings. With a total of some two hundred employees at both processing plants, in the end Mizue left the matter of the New Year's party entirely up to her husband.

In addition to the two managers, there were about six senior staff at the processing plants who came to the house. As she was warming saké for them, Mizue wondered why they went through this same ritual every year. She herself never enjoyed it. She had married into a well-to-do family so perhaps she could afford to look down on it all. Or perhaps her thoughts reflected the monotony of her life. Every year at the New Year's party several female employees would assist her in the kitchen, and this year too five showed up.

All the visitors admired the garden and made the exact same comment: that it was very nice, and that it looked like a garden in one of the Kyoto temples.

But of course it was not such a simple garden. Kase had carefully posi-tioned the stones so that, after the leaves had fallen from the trees, the bare branches would indicate the role the trees played in the composition of the whole garden. Mizue realized now that her husband was not aware of these subtleties. While Kase was building the garden she had seen him go time and again to the front gate to see how it looked from there. He had also viewed the garden from inside the house. Where there were too many trees, he had dug some up and transplanted them.

Now Mizue realized why he had been so careful. The garden was not very large. But whether viewed from the front gate or from the house, when the trees had all their leaves it gave the impression of a forest. After the leaves had fallen, you could clearly see the boundaries of the garden, so Kase had arranged things in such a way that you would not be conscious of its size. On entering the gate in winter, the first thing you noticed was the stately shapes of the bare trees and stones. They drew your atten-tion so you did not bother to look as far as the hedge. Only after a while did you then notice the winter camellias in the hedge. Since these had been thinned while still in bud, their red color attracted attention from a distance. But they did not dominate the scene, and as you gazed at the garden, the far-off background of the red flowers revealed how trees and strategically placed stones lay at the very core of the garden design. It all had a very natural appearance.

"It is surprising to find a house built like this so that it doesn't destroy the natural beauty of the mountains," one of the visitors from the compa-ny commented to Shida. It struck Mizue that this was the result of Kase's magic. Viewed from one perspective, nature is really chaos, but this gar-den, while retaining that disorder, expressed a natural sort of beauty and contained nothing superfluous.

The New Year's gathering passed uneventfully and soon the holiday spirit subsided. Mizue visited the main house in Kugenuma to pay her own New Year's respects, and finally January came to an end.

On the afternoon of the first Monday in February Shida brought guests home. Members of the prefectural Cultural Properties Commission, they said the Shida garden was situated on land that had once been a road, and that there should be two ancient stone statues of roadside deities on the property. They had come to investigate. Mizue recalled that while Kase had been building the garden he had indeed found some stone Buddhas; since they were obviously old, he had decided to leave them as they were. They were in a corner of the grove of trees.

All three members of the Cultural Properties Commission were gentlemen in their fifties or older.

"What a natural-looking garden!" one of them commented.

"Not at all," said another. "This is a properly made garden. It was not just any gardener who did this. This is superb."

The third member of the group asked Shida who had designed and built the garden. Shida mentioned Kase's name.

"It is quite remarkable to find a garden like this these days. Architects today usually create some showy thing to express their egos, but this garden is not like that; it has the refined grace of *shibumi*. It reminds me of how the tea ceremony was early on, before the innovations of Furuta Oribe. It's not flashy and it's not modern."

Mizue learned later that this man was a scholar who had published books on Zen, the tea ceremony, and gardens, and that he rejected gardens and tea ware that reflected modern tastes; to him anything from the seventeenth century on was modern.

Mizue had not observed the garden to the extent that she appreciated its subtle grace and understated beauty. Until now it had just seemed ordinary without being commonplace. It had not been a garden of hidden meanings. But now her new perception of the garden opened up new levels of feeling, and she began to re-examine her emotions.

2

As winter gave way to spring the bare trees were at their most beautiful. This is how Kase had envisioned the trees. Their beauty lay in their lack of ostentation, and then in the way they began to put forth buds in spring. Evergreens were also beautiful, but in a different way; they lacked the purity of deciduous trees. Evergreens continually grew and renewed themselves, but deciduous trees died and were reborn.

In the garden behind Kase's apartment building was a large hardwood tree. Its trunk was some two feet in diameter, and its top reached nearly to the fifth floor windows. This tree stood resolute in the midst of the desolate city. It had probably been battered many times by various pieces of machinery while the apartments were being built, and it still bore scars here and there, but its straight trunk and lofty branches were unaffected. After gazing at this natural tree, Kase found the art of making miniature bonsai trees meager and impoverished, and somehow disagreeable. For Kase, of course, the great hardwood tree and the tiny bonsai were simply metaphors. In every small, closed world, there is the same quality of complacency and exclusiveness.

I suppose I should show up at the office in Shibuya tomorrow, thought Kase, for it was already ten days into the new year. It was like this every year. The same things happened over and over and all he ever accomplished each year was a few more gardens. What he felt especially bad about was that he had made several dry landscape—*karesansui*—gardens. There is nothing more haphazard than the random meanings suggested to the viewer by a dry landscape garden containing nothing but stone arrangements, gravel, and perhaps some moss or other low plantings. Its effect is like some sort of irrational magic. Kase felt his *karesansui* were even fraudulent or deceptive.

Dry landscape gardens represent landscapes without the use of water. They center around groups of stones, and where water elements are needed they use sand or gravel instead. According to legends that have been passed down, these dry gardens were first created by Zen priests under the influence of Chinese Sung and Ming dynasty landscape paintings. Though Kase was not a strict believer in Zen, he had created several rock gardens in his own fashion. Even after researching the matter, however, it was still not clear to him what connections might exist between Zen koans and dry landscape gardens. He had started building dry landscapes five years ago. A year before that he had spent a month traveling in Korea. There he had been able to see both dry gardens and landscape paintings as they actually existed in nature. After this, his reluctance to do dry landscape gardens disappeared and he confidently responded to requests to design them.

Still, for anyone who has seen "real" dry landscapes in nature, an artificially created garden would not do. It was when looking at the Daisenin garden in Kyoto that Kase felt he really understood what Japanese temple gardens were all about. He found the Daisenin garden completely artificial; while its miniature landscape of a waterfall, cliffs, and spreading sea closely imitated nature, the idea was immaturely expressed. Zen was not necessary to appreciate Daisenin. Anyone could see it just as it was. Kase, however, could never build such a garden.

On Mount Sokrisan in Korea stands the Bopjusa Temple. Kase's hotel was at the foot of the mountain, and when he looked out his window at the ground rising up behind, he was startled to discover the basic model of a landscape painting. There on that mountain slope with no intervention of human artifice were stones, red pines, and a flowing river with a bed of white gravel. The river bed was dry, of course, but it was clear that whenever it rained the water would flow. The combination of stones, red pines, and a river bed—this is exactly what constitutes a landscape painting.

Kase was also unable to create a garden like the one at the Jishoji temple in Kyoto, with its raked sand waves and its mound of sand that is said to look like a full moon. Legend has it that this garden was the creation of Shinso, a landscape painter and tea master of the Muromachi period, and that Shinso designed the wildly abstract garden at the Ryoanji temple as well. Kase thought these contentions absurd. Those looking for something richly evocative in a garden can find it, while those looking for random and irregular elements can find them there, too.

Nor was Kase satisfied by the gardens done in the Yamato-e style, such as the pond and hillside garden at the Tenryuji temple in Kyoto. Its cluster of stones in the middle of the pond—the idea, perhaps, of some Zen priest—seemed out of place. Still, seen as a whole, the garden was pure Yamato-style: flat and smooth and much too pretty. It was clearly a garden of the late courtly period and looked like it had been constructed according to rules laid down in some manual on garden building, like a stage set.

Kase recollected how he had first become interested in gardens in his early twenties and had traveled around looking at famous examples. He retained strong impressions of several of these, and had gone on to build gardens he was satisfied with.

A good garden cannot be made without exploiting the contours of the land. Kase was unable to create Zen-style gardens that used only clusters of stone. Such gardens by modern landscape architects always struck a false note. Kase could do no more than design simple dry landscapes to represent mountains and water.

But what about the garden he had made for the Shidas? It was not in the pretty Yamato-e style, nor was it a Zen-style dry landscape. It was merely an extension of nature as nature actually existed. Had the garden, he wondered, aroused some feelings in Mizue?

Kase spent the first ten days of the new year at a hotel and then at his apartment, his mind filled with thoughts like these. On the morning of the eleventh he set out for Tokyo and his office in Shibuya.

3

Momoko, the maid, was from Udoko just north of Atsugi. Every summer at the time of the Buddhist Festival, Mizue would send her home for a visit to her family. But this year, early in February, word came that Momoko's mother was dying, and she returned home. This was two days after the members of the Cultural Properties Commission had come to examine the old roadside statues in the garden.

The village of Udoko was on the banks of the Nakatsu River and had once been a center for the production of Japanese handmade paper. In the fall three years ago, Mizue had made an excursion up the Nakatsu River gorge to view the autumn leaves and visit the home of Momoko's family, who themselves had once been paper makers. Momoko had come to work for the Shidas right after graduating from high school and had been with them now for seven years. Mizue felt it was time to begin looking for a suitable husband for her. She had spoken to Shida about the matter several times since the beginning of the year.

Momoko returned to the Shidas' after an absence of five days. Hearing the buzzer at the kitchen door, Mizue opened it to find Momoko standing there. "I'm back. Mother had already passed away from a heart attack by the time I reached home. But she was seventy and died peacefully. We've already had the funeral." Momoko was no longer grieving.

Before Momoko entered the house, Mizue took a small handful of salt and sprinkled it over her in the traditional ritual of purification. "We have been intending to go and offer incense ever since we heard."

"The temple is quite close by car; I would be pleased if you would go when it is convenient. Oh, by the way, I saw Mr. Kase yesterday."

"Mr. Kase? At Udoko?"

"Many people around there have nurseries and raise seedlings. He said he was in the area to buy alpine trees."

When she said alpine trees, Mizue wondered if that meant trees growing wild in the mountains. Her mind went back to the comment made by one of the members of the Cultural Properties Commission that the garden did not have a modern feel about it; he had compared it to the tea ceremony, saying that like the tea style prior to the innovations of Oribe, it was not gaudy.

That evening when her husband returned home, Mizue told him about the death of Momoko's mother. "I'll be expected to go and offer incense. Won't you come too? It's quite close if we go by car."

"I can go tomorrow; shall we go together?"

"The day after tomorrow will be the seventh day after her passing," Mizue said. "If we wait until then, we won't have to wear mourning clothes."

"That doesn't matter. You get a new bank note to give as a funerary offering. Tomorrow morning I'll go to the Hiratsuka plant and be back about noon; we can go then."

The next day, after a simple lunch, Shida and his wife set out for Udoko.

They stopped off at the plant at Atsugi for about twenty minutes and arrived at Momoko's home on the bank of the Nakatsu River shortly before three o'clock. Momoko's eldest brother was the head of the family now. They grew greenhouse vegetables and raised seedlings on the side.

The Shidas looked around, but there was no sign of anyone at the house. "Maybe they're working in the fields," said Shida, walking around the house.

Mizue looked down at the river from the yard. She wondered if there were families in the village who still made paper. A few hundred yards downstream she could see some yellow-white fibers being bleached in the river. They were surely some kind of mulberry bark, the basic staple in traditional handmade paper. A small obstruction had been built to stop the flow of water just where the fibers were bleaching, but there was no one around. Oblique rays of winter sun struck the surface of the water and created a serene mood. At Atsugi downstream, the Nakatsu River muddied the Sagami River, but here at this small village the river was clear. Mizue could see every stone and pebble on the bottom.

"There doesn't seem to be anyone in the fields out back either," said Shida, returning. He had found plastic trays for growing lettuce and long plastic quonsets covering rows of vegetables, but no sign of any people.

"Shall we wait here for a while and see if anyone shows up?"

"Let's wait just long enough for me to smoke a cigarette. I need to be back at the plant at three-thirty."

The sliding glass doors at the side of the house were open, so they sat on the edge of the raised veranda. "I wonder if they are still making hand-made paper around here."

"Apparently there is only one family left that does. But I hear they are going to build a dam upstream in the near future, and when that happens they won't be able to make paper anymore. In the old days this river was even purer than it is now." Shida was referring to a time long ago when he had come here camping.

Mizue felt there was something strange about this village. The whole place felt dusty despite the presence of the river. Situated as it was on the eastern slope of the Tanzawa range, the land here seemed open and unprotected. Perhaps it was just that all the trees in the surrounding forest had dropped their leaves for the winter.

"There's no way we can get in touch with them. Shall we go?"

Shida tore a sheet from his pocket notebook and wrote that they had made their offering from the veranda. He attached the note to the envelope they had brought and left it there. Then both husband and wife stood for a moment facing the house, hands clasped in prayer.

They came out onto the road that follows the right bank of the river and soon reached the highway connecting Atsugi and Tsukui. They turned left there. From the car window Mizue gazed out at the brown, withered landscape and wondered where Momoko had met Kase.

When they reached the plant at Atsugi, Shida went inside while Mizue waited in the car. A moment later one of the plant employees came out and drove her home to Hadano.

All the way to Udoko and back Mizue's eyes had searched for a landscape that resembled the garden Kase had built for her. She was not looking for exactly the same shape and structure. But since the beginning of the year she had found herself making the same search every time she went out. There was no reason to expect to find this sort of fragmented landscape in the natural world. Yet the garden Kase had built was always before her eyes, and Mizue had made it a symbol, reading into it the true object of her yearning. That day when the Cultural Properties Commission member had praised the garden, Mizue began to fear the direction her feelings were taking. It was then, for the first time, that she looked inside herself and knew what she was searching for.

4

An acquaintance of Kase's, a builder, had constructed a small one-story house occupying 1,800 square feet on the outskirts of Tokyo. Toward the end of the previous year he had asked Kase to build a garden on the property's remaining 4,500 square feet that would highlight the trees already growing there. When Kase went to inspect the site, he found a street along the north side of the property, traditional Japanese-style wooden houses on both sides, and a two-story reinforced concrete house on the south. Kase's friend's house was on the west side of the property, leaving the east and south open for a garden. The houses on both sides and the one to the south were all surrounded by iron fences.

The problem was the concrete house to the south. It was large, and in order to make a proper barrier that would provide privacy for his friend's house it would be necessary to put in an evergreen hedge. But since the house was not really bad-looking, Kase suggested a mixture of deciduous and evergreen trees. In summer the concrete house would be completely screened off, but in winter when the leaves had fallen one would have glimpses of it through the branches. Kase's friend agreed with this suggestion.

Kase had met the maid Momoko on the street in Udoko when he had gone there to buy trees for this garden. It was essential that the trees be transplanted in January or February. February was best; if they were transplanted then and watered well until the middle of March, most of the trees would be putting out buds in April and May.

For Kase the contours of a landscape were as identifiable as a person's features. Reducing those features in size and transferring them whole to a garden was like making a bonsai. That did not make a garden. Kase's method was to isolate a single feature of the landscape and then re-create it in the garden.

He had spent two days walking through the Tanzawa mountains searching out trees and deciding which ones he wanted for the garden. He was accompanied by Heizo, who raised trees up around Ogino. Their route took them north from Ogino, and it was when they had come down from the mountains on the afternoon of the second day and were following the road along the Nakatsu River that a girl going the opposite direction had called out, "Oh! Mr. Kase." This was Momoko. Kase remembered the cheerful girl who had been at the Shidas' house when he had built the garden there, but the Momoko he met at Udoko was far more attractive. With no evident distress she announced that she had come home for her mother's funeral.

When he asked her how things were with the Shidas, she replied cheerfully, "Oh, everything is just fine there."

He wondered how the garden was developing, but decided it would be pointless to ask Momoko. Instead he asked her to say hello to the Shidas and went on his way. Normally a garden builder can review his progress by comparing the garden he has actually built to the vision of it in his mind. Kase had not been able to do that with the Shidas' garden, because the true object of his vision there was Mizue.

He could not honestly say that the garden for his friend's house was based on a vision he had in his mind. He had made his best effort, but it was somehow less than perfect. Kase discussed this problem with his friend and suggested they wait a year and try again. The friend, however, was completely satisfied with the way things were going. He owned a construction company with offices in downtown Tokyo, and only returned home to the suburbs to sleep anyway. When he got up in the morning he wanted to be able to look out at the garden while he drank his tea. If he had a garden adequate for that, it would be good enough. Kase completed the garden by the end of March.

After finishing, Kase spent a week at his apartment in Hodogaya working on plans for a new garden. He had been hired by a traditional Japanese-style painter who had had a house in Tokyo before moving back to the familiar mountains of his native village in Yamagata, far to the northwest, where he had decided to spend the rest of his days. His home there was near the Risshakuji temple, and he had nearly half an acre of open land on which to build a garden. The ground was very uneven and faced the river. It was just the kind of job a landscape architect liked to do, and while Kase worked on the plans he had combination breakfasts and lunches sent in from a nearby restaurant and went out each night for dinner.

Later, the doorbell rang as he was drinking his tea. He thought it was the restaurant bringing his noon meal, but when he opened the door, there stood his ex-wife Emiko. Radiant in a cream suit, she seemed to have brought spring with her.

"You should see the expression on your face," said Emiko, entering the room. "You make me feel unwelcome."

"No. It's just that you're wearing that light-colored suit. I was about to say you look terrific."

As Emiko sat down on the sofa, the buzzer rang once again. This time it was the restaurant. Kase carried the two-tiered lunch box to the dining room table and asked Emiko if she would like to share it with him.

"I've already eaten, thank you. I phoned your office in Shibuya yesterday; they told me you would be staying here for a while, so I had an early breakfast this morning before I came. You need someone to take care of you. Why don't you get married again?"

"That's a foolish question."

"I guess you've learned your lesson after two failed marriages. I'll bet you have another woman, a married woman, who's been seeing you here."

"Unfortunately, my dear, you're the only one right now."

"I find that hard to believe, since you don't even see me once a month."

"Men aren't the lustful animals that women are."

One tray of the lunch box contained rice, the other vegetables, and such savory foods as fried shrimp, grilled fish, boiled beef, fried eggs, boiled pumpkin and taro, and clams. It was the same meal every day, varying only in the type of fried food and the grilled fish.

"Do you have your evening meal sent in too?"

"No, I go out for dinner."

As he picked the fish apart with his chopsticks, Kase wondered how long it had been since Emiko had come to him and began to count the days. The last time had probably been around the twentieth of March. His ex-wife had first returned to him in the winter three years ago. At that time he had lost his head over this thirty-year-old woman. Emiko had been twenty-five when she left Kase, and he looked back over the years and months she had been someone else's wife; she had not remained free from him for very long. He envied the sexual confidence he had observed in other men. But after he had been with Emiko several times, their relationship became purely sexual. She lived in Kawasaki now. Her husband was an accountant, and Emiko had once told Kase that in a few years he was going to run as a candidate for city council.

As he finished eating, he heard Emiko open the door to the bedroom. Although he enjoyed having a woman, recently Kase had come to prefer that she leave right away. He never felt satisfied afterward.

5

The day Kase completed the front garden, he had had a talk with Shida in which he murmured self-consciously that for him making a garden was a struggle against mediocrity. Now as Mizue looked out at the budding trees she wondered what he had meant. It had been in March, already over a year ago, that work had begun on the garden. Mizue wondered whether Kase would ever come here again. As her days passed in weary

45

succession, Kase's garden consoled her, but it was not the same as actually hearing him speak to her. She wanted to hear once more the sound of his voice that came to her like the wind blowing among stones on a barren mountain. Mizue realized the danger in this feeling. Yet even in her wildest fantasy she did not allow herself to go all the way. As long as she was in this house, she would painfully stem the natural flow of her emotions. Pain and desire mingled, became inseparable, and there were days when, looking out at the garden, she felt the full weight of her malaise.

As the buds on the trees continued to swell, deepening in color day by day, so did Mizue's own feelings cut a deeper shadow.

A short distance from the Shidas' home was a farm where flowers were raised. Each Monday Mizue had flowers delivered. One Monday morning toward the end of April she saw her husband and children off and phoned the farm to say she would come herself to pick up the flowers. In the mornings and evenings the Shida garden was transformed as its colors heightened, and at these times especially Mizue felt the garden was watching her. She spoke to herself as she walked to the farm. I wonder if people would really understand if I told them being watched by the garden exhausts me, but it's true.

She had walked to the farm many times before, but today Mizue was astounded by the number and variety of flowers. There was a row of four greenhouses as she entered the farm yard. In front of the one on the far right were the family's eldest son and his wife. They were loading their small truck with stacks of flowers wrapped in straw matting.

"Why, Mrs. Shida, please come in. You didn't have to walk all the way down here." The wife removed the towel she was using to cover her head and bowed a greeting to Mizue.

"I don't mind. It's a lovely day for a walk. What sort of flowers do you have today?"

"We have peonies. Or how about some clematis?" asked the eldest son.

"Fine. I'll have ten of the peonies. What about the clematis, are they potted or cut?"

"They're cut."

"I guess I'll take a few of those as well. These white flowers you have wrapped in straw are pretty too."

"These are a tropical plant called pyramidalis." The eldest son got into the truck. "Excuse me, Mrs. Shida, I have to go into town now. My wife will cut your flowers for you." They were a good-natured couple who had two small children.

The truck departed and Mizue accompanied the wife into the greenhouse. All the windows were open and in one corner was a profusion of peonies.

"Would you like half of them in white and half in red?"

"I think I'd like seven white ones and three red."

The wife cut ten flowers, mixing several that were just budding with some in full bloom. She laid the flowers out on her worktable and tapped each stalk with the handle of her shears so it would absorb water more readily and remain fresh longer.

"The clematis are in the other greenhouse." The wife wrapped the peonies in straw and placed them in a long, thin wicker basket, then led Mizue next door. Inside were potted clematis that would be ready for shipping in a couple of weeks.

The wife cut several of the flowers for Mizue. "Go ahead and take the basket with you. I can pick it up next time I deliver flowers to your place."

Mizue took the basket and flowers and returned home. She placed the peonies in a foot-tall Shigaraki vase and set it on the flagstone floor just inside the front door of the house. One of the clematis she put in a tall thin Bizen vase which she placed in the tea room. She put the other in a Korean vase from the Yi dynasty and placed it on the mirror stand in her own room. The Korean vase was glazed white china, a memento from her father.

Mizue returned to the tea room and set about the complex ritual of preparing ceremonial tea for herself. They would be using a portable brazier in the tea room throughout the summer months. As she served the tea, Mizue gazed out at the garden that presented itself to view and wondered what Kase had meant when he had spoken of his struggle against mediocrity.

Mizue felt trapped. She had arranged flowers and had performed tea ceremony, but nothing helped to calm the torrent of her emotions.

The next morning at breakfast she announced to her husband that she would be going into Tokyo that day to the Ginza. Since she had only two fresh pairs of traditional summer tabi socks left, she had ordered more from a shop in the Ginza in early April; a few days earlier they had called to say her order was ready.

"While you're in the city, will you buy some pipe tobacco for me?" Shida asked. He enjoyed smoking a pipe around the house, but in rural Hadano he could not buy imported tobacco.

Mizue saw her husband and children off, then got ready to go. After some indecision about what to wear, she took from the drawer a finely woven, gray-blue kimono. Its gray background was decorated with a delicate pattern of chrysanthemums in crimson. Her obi was a plain mustard color. Mizue had inherited her elegant and restrained taste from her father.

Rather than take the private train line to Shinjuku and then transferring, she preferred to take the bus to Hiratsuka and the national railway from there right into downtown Tokyo. The tabi shop she wanted was located in the heart of the Ginza district. She had shopped there for many years, since the days she had lived in Oiso. She picked up her dozen pairs of summer tabi and then went on to a tobacconist's, where she bought five cans of tobacco.

Mizue enjoyed the time she spent doing these errands. There was a gentle pleasure in being busy with something that did not involve her emotionally. It was past one o'clock when she came out of the tobacco shop. She still had not made up her mind whether or not to see Kase. His office was on Sakuragaoka Street; she had looked it up on her husband's map of Tokyo. It was located a few minutes' walk from Shibuya Station, across town.

To Mizue, for a woman to call on a man seemed extraordinary behavior. Still, she remembered that day the previous summer when she had met Kase on her way to the cemetery at Oiso. He had told her he remembered seeing her when she was eighteen. That must have been some sort of declaration. Perhaps he felt he could not say anything more than that to a married woman with two children.

Mizue boarded the subway. Later, standing in front of the building that housed Kase's office, Mizue, at the age of thirty-three, was still confident of her innocence. After getting off the subway at Shibuya, she had stopped at a department store in the terminal building and bought a bottle of Bulgarian cognac. The gift would provide an excuse for her visit.

Kase's offices were on the third floor. The young receptionist told Mizue that Kase was downstairs in the coffee shop and phoned him for her.

Kase appeared moments later.

"I was in Tokyo doing some errands, so I decided to stop in. Our garden is just putting out new spring growth, and . . ." Without finishing the sentence, Mizue merely held out the bottle of cognac.

"Shall we go down to the coffee shop?" Kase held the door open for her. They took the stairs down rather than the elevator.

"Have you eaten lunch yet?" asked Kase as they reached the lobby.

"Yes, thank you."

Why don't we just have coffee then."

"No, thank you. Not coffee. Perhaps we could just walk together for a few minutes instead."

Kase did not reply. They walked up a hill and paused in front of a school building.

"Every day I have the feeling I'm being watched by your garden. Did you intend it that way?"

Kase stood looking into the school yard. "Do you trust the garden?"

"Do I have any choice?"

"I'm glad you feel this way. I consider it a compliment. I meant to give you up if the garden did not succeed. As it turns out now I have no chance to see the garden and visit you."

"That can't be helped, can it?"

"In a few days I'll be going off to Yamagata Prefecture. I'll probably be there for three months. Of course I'll be making occasional trips back to Tokyo."

"I'm glad."

Though Mizue's desperate feelings were quite real, until now they had been vague and indistinct. Now that at last she could be with Kase, everything seemed to come into focus, to become simple, yet rich with possibilities. Not everyone, Mizue reflected, would like Kase's garden. It is not a question of whether he was true to his art in building it; for him, the point of making a garden is to struggle against mediocrity. Knowing this, I can decide for myself whether his garden suits me or not.

"I suppose you weren't expecting this?"

"On the contrary, there was no other way it could have happened. Just as you couldn't help coming here today. The only thing I cared about in designing that garden was how to arouse you."

At that moment a crowd of school children came running around one corner of the building; they appeared to be third or fourth graders. Mizue was reminded of her own daughter, Noriko.

"From now on I won't be able to feel quite so innocent in that house. And yet, I can always feel perfectly innocent when I'm with you. Please believe me."

"I believe you."

"Well, I have to be going. Will you telephone me before you leave for Yamagata?"

"Certainly."

They returned down the slope they had just climbed and parted at the bottom.

Returning to Shibuya Station, Mizue took the train to Shimo-Kitazawa, and by the time she had transferred there she felt overcome by that pleasant fatigue that follows a period of intense strain.

6

Building a garden, in Kase's case, was also a struggle with himself. Too often, rather than be creative, artists are content merely to make statements that draw attention to themselves. Kase's thinking was that a work of art need not be idiosyncratic just because it has been filtered through the subjective view of the artist. When he had come to the Shidas' house and met Mizue for the second time, what passed through Kase's mind was that she was just like a stone that enhances a bland landscape. It was the first time in his career that he had had such a feeling. More than anything else, Kase was relieved that Mizue, unlike any other women he had known, seemed refreshing and wholesome. In his struggle against mediocrity, she was the only woman he could ever have encountered.

After eating a late dinner in Shibuya, Kase returned to his Hodogaya apartment and showered. As he sipped a final drink before going to bed, he thought about his meeting with Mizue that afternoon.

Why is it we make such a nicely balanced pair? Kase thought. What is the bond we share; is it like a stone, or like a tree? Whatever, there's no question that my garden has aroused her feelings.

Kase's mood as he sipped his drink was one of supreme satisfaction.

At ten o'clock the next morning Kase arrived at his office. Almost immediately there was a phone call from Emiko. She said she would come see him around noon. Whenever she came to him at the office, it was their custom to use one of the hourly rooms at a nearby love hotel.

"I can't manage it today," said Kase.

"Why not? What's wrong with you today?"

"I'm busy."

"That's too bad, because I won't be able to make it tomorrow. Why can't you find some time today?"

She was the sort who always wanted immediate gratification. Back in the days when they were married, she had been this way about other things as well. Kase felt it was inevitable that he would soon stop seeing Emiko.

"All right, all right. I understand."

"Good. About noon then. I'll be waiting at the usual place."

The usual place was a hotel on a small side street off Dogenzaka, the main street up from the station. Kase wondered idly how many times he had met Emiko there, and he was not excited about meeting her there again today. Sex with her had become boring and repetitive. When he thought of the futility he always felt afterward the idea of going became even more distasteful to him.

Kase left his office shortly before noon and headed reluctantly toward the rendezvous. He crossed a pedestrian bridge and came out in front of the post office at Dogenzaka. Walking through the early summer sunshine, he thought about the garden he had built for the Shidas. There had never been a garden quite like it, not even in the old garden manuals. These works attached great significance to having a pond, but Kase had declined to put one in, even though the Shidas' garden was relatively spacious. According to the old manual known as the "Illustrations," "When digging a pond, its shape must resemble the wide ocean, and its manner must resemble the course of a flowing river." Yet, no matter how one imitated the patterns of nature, one could never make a garden pond resemble the wide ocean or the flowing of a river. Behind the Shida garden towered the Tanzawa massif, and in front was the Kaneme River. In such a grand setting nothing would be gained by trying to create a miniature pond. If he could have channeled a natural stream through the garden, he would have done so, but the Shidas' home stood too high above the river, making that impossible.

In the *Sakuteiki,* as well, it says, "It is important for each home to have a spring. With a spring one can find refuge from the heat." How foolish, Kase thought. The *Sakuteiki* was reliable only on the subject of placing stones. The rest was nonsense, even when it dealt with planting trees.

Kase imagined Mizue standing in the garden colored with its growth of new foliage. This was not like some dream of a far-distant world; it was immediate and real. Mizue's figure seemed to blend into the trees that grew upward and upward, forever. It was the same with the stones erected in the garden. Summer and autumn, winter and spring, they changed their appearance with the changing seasons. And as they changed, Mizue merged with the trees and the stones and finally dissolved into infinity.

Did I alone as an architect design and build this garden, Kase wondered, or did this woman Mizue cause it to be built?

This reverie was enormously pleasing to Kase. At the moment, however, he had to deal with the reality of his sexual encounter with Emiko. Kase stopped right before he reached the hotel; he wished there were some way to retreat. Emiko had first visited him at Hodogaya in the winter some three years ago, but the next time she had called his office saying she was at Shibuya Station. They had met at a coffee shop and afterward had come to this place. It had been a cold winter day, and this street had inspired in him a feeling of poetic desolation; now, however, the street before him merely seemed sleazy and grimy. He gazed at the hotel sign and in it he saw all the ugliness of lust. Not only Emiko's lust, but his own, which was no different from hers.

I wonder if Mizue can purify such physical desire, he thought.

WATER

(The Garden at Tenryuji)

1

On a day in spring when the new leaves were deepening in color, Mizue began to examine her situation. She was a wife and a mother more than thirty years old. She had two children. How had she gotten herself into this emotional state? What was it like for other women? Were these feelings of hers real?

Now that Kase had gone to Yamagata, Mizue could see clearly that her impulses were more than simply sexual desire. Two days after their first meeting in Shibuya, the day before his departure to Yamagata, Mizue had met Kase again. High above Shinjuku on the twentieth floor of a hotel, where the silence belied the activity of the streets below, Mizue had surrendered to the flow of her emotions. Kase was a stone that had been dropped into the current of her feelings. As Kase buried himself within her she saw the monotonous world of her present life collapsing. There was nothing wasted in this experience. They had arrived at the hotel shortly after noon and did not leave until four o'clock. On the train home she wondered if what she had experienced was the full vitality of a creative artist.

Nearly half a month had passed since that day. In the meantime Mizue's husband continued to enjoy his elegant pleasures and find time in his busy work schedule for refined diversions. Five days after her encounter with Kase it occurred to Mizue that the cool aloofness with which she now regarded her husband was a form of cruelty.

Shida constantly extolled his garden, saying how wonderful it had become. Mizue was almost envious. Ah, he has no idea what suffering is, she thought. What a wonderful way to live!

As the green foliage in the garden increased, it became more difficult to see the stones from the house. But Mizue was aware of the exact location of each stone in the garden. It now seemed to her that nothing was so true as those stones.

Over a period of time every happy family establishes its own routines, and Mizue had been thinking how routine her own life had become until Kase had appeared the year before. The night she returned from the hotel, she wondered what it would be like to spend all her days with Kase. And yet Mizue had no desire to break up her family. Her frozen emotions flowed again and she felt cleansed.

2

New spring foliage was slower to appear in Yamagata than in Tokyo or Hadano to the south, but now it was May and the country around the Risshakuji temple was radiant with spring. The painter's house was almost completed; the old man had arrived there from Tokyo only half a month earlier. The house was a traditional one-story building covering about 2,500 square feet. Kase was staying in a six-tatami-mat room on the east side. The two students who accompanied him from Tokyo occupied an adjoining six-tatami-mat room.

The rainy season would be upon them by the middle of June, so they would have to finish placing the trees before then. As at the Shidas' garden, Kase planned to use the natural slope of the land, but while the Shidas' garden was 7,000 square feet, this one in Yamagata was well over twice that size. In the limited space of the Shidas' garden Kase could intensify everything. The problem here was how to maintain that same quality of intensity on a much larger scale.

The artist who owned the property was a bit past sixty and had spent all his life painting scenes from nature in the Japanese style. "I'd like to add some touches to the garden that didn't appear in the plans I showed you," Kase said to him one morning at breakfast.

"That's fine with me. I won't complain unless you make the garden look really obvious."

"There is also the problem of channeling water into the garden from the river. What shall we do about that? If we want to divert river water, we'll have to make an application to the authorities for permission."

"What do you think we should do?"

"At first I thought it'd be a good idea to bring water into the garden and I designed it that way, but after actually spending time here, I think things are fine just as they are. The view of the river itself can be considered a part of the garden."

"In that case let's not bother bringing the stream in."

"The ground slopes down to the river, and I'd like to thin out some of the forest there so you can see the river through the trees."

When Kase had first arrived in March to inspect the site, he did think it would be best to channel a stream through the garden. But he became afraid that if they brought a stream in, it would dwarf everything else. A number of red pines grew on the east side of the garden in a grove that extended up the side of the mountain. There was also a fairly dense stand of pine and other trees along the river bank, including several varieties of birch. The type called Soro birch had an attractive trunk; when pruned properly it would make for a very elegant garden tree, particularly in winter when it had lost its leaves and the trunk was especially prominent.

The entrance to the artist's house was on the west side. A patch of dwarf bamboo here had been dug out when the house was built, so this area was barren of trees. Kase thought he would bring in some of the pines from the east side of the house.

In 1735, Kitamura Enkin published a garden manual called *Tsukiyama Niwazukuri-den,* or "Teachings on the Construction of Landscape Gardens." In this work he recorded the following, as part of the secret oral gardening tradition:

> It is best to plant pine trees in the second month of the year. Since pines dislike too much moisture, the bottom of the hole should be lined with charcoal dust and leaves. Pressed *konnyaku* potato must be placed on the roots. From time to time it is best to boil some *senkyu* watercress, and after it has cooled to put this tea on the roots.

The "second month of the year" corresponds to the modern month of March. Charcoal dust and *senkyu*—a medicinal herb related to parsley—were routinely used, not only for pines, but for transplanting any tree. The function of the *konnyaku* is not clear.

Although he had not yet done so, Kase had considered doing some experiments along these lines. The "Teachings" gave the following method for restoring a pine tree:

> If the pine tree is already changing color and you do not wish it to wither, dig the tree up and trim the small roots slightly with a saw. Wrap the cut portions with dried cuttlefish; tie this down with straw and replant the tree. The main root, however, should be left alone. If these instructions are followed, the tree will revive and turn green again. These instructions are to be kept secret.

Such methods sounded silly, but it was possible that this gardener from olden times was correct. Since two pines on the east side of the artist's house were beginning to wither, one day Kase suggested to his students that they try some dried cuttlefish on them.

"Are you serious?" asked one of the students in disbelief.

"You don't often find pines in this condition. This is a good opportunity to see if the old formula works. Later I want you to go into town and buy some dried cuttlefish."

"You're getting a bit eccentric, to try something like this."

"I also want you to check with the people here and see if they have any charcoal. If not, buy some of that too."

"I think it's a waste of time, but if you insist, I'll do it. But surely you're not going to experiment with both trees, are you?"

"We'll do it with both trees."

After lunch, one of the students took the truck and went to town to buy the dried cuttlefish. They spent the rest of the afternoon treating and transplanting the withered pines. Next to the river, they found a place to crush the charcoal, mix it with dead leaves, and prepare a bed for the transplanted trees.

That evening at dinner they talked about the pines with the painter, who was especially interested when Kase explained how they had used the dried cuttlefish. The painter lived there with only his wife and two maids from the nearby town of Sagae. His children, he said, were grown and preferred to live in Tokyo.

The following morning Kase requested the help of three gardeners from a local nursery. He asked them to thin out the trees along the river bank, taking all the small ones, leaving only the strong.

"Can you have the job done in ten days?" Kase asked the oldest of the three, a man of about fifty who acted as foreman of the crew.

"Sure," he replied, "Ten days is fine."

While the local gardeners were busy along the river bank, Kase moved the red pines from the east to the west side of the house. There were some forty pines in all, from ten to fifteen feet in height. He selected ten of them for transplanting.

During the afternoon, while charring the ends of the cedar poles they would use to brace up the transplanted trees, they heard several times the song of nightingales. During the mornings, they had heard the nightingales in this same place, warbling for an hour or two at a time. By the time they had tied the cedar poles to the trees, the sun was setting.

The next morning, as he was walking in the garden before breakfast, Kase heard the song of a cuckoo coming from the direction of the mountains. Near at hand he could hear the songs of nightingales and turtledoves, but very faintly in the distance, he heard the call of the cuckoo. This was the first time since coming here that he had heard the bird, and it made him wonder if there was a larch grove nearby—the favorite haunt of the cuckoo. All around on three sides were mountains at least three thousand feet high, so it would not be surprising to find larch forests here.

This is a perfect morning, thought Kase, gazing at the mountains. In a flood he felt himself wanting to share it with Mizue, to have her experience it too. Being with her was like having total experience of another person. He had known many women—Emiko, for example, and before her others—but this was the first time Kase had known a woman he could share his feelings with so completely, one who could understand his inmost thoughts and feelings and whose thoughts and feelings he could understand. If Eiji Shida ever wanted proof that Kase's relationship with Mizue was completely satisfying, he believed he could offer that proof.

"Did you hear the cuckoo this morning?" asked the painter at breakfast.

"Yes, I heard it."

"He always shows up about this time of year and stays until early October."

"Is there a larch forest nearby?"

"Yes, there is, but recently the cuckoos have been living in other places as well. If you climb to the mountain temple, you can hear them there, too. You know, of course, that cuckoos don't build their own nests. When it's time to lay their eggs, they use the nest of some other bird, the shrike, the bunting, the kylar, or the wagtail. They'll lay many nests with suitable parent birds. That's why they can't live exclusively in larch forests."

"This is the first time I've heard they don't make nests of their own."

"They're clever birds; cunning, really. When they're ready to lay their eggs, they go to the other bird's nest and drop one of the eggs out of it and replace it with one of their own. Their eggs are speckled, like those of a shrike or bunting." The old painter said that, since his youth, he had spent much time rambling in the mountains sketching, and that consequently he was familiar with the habits of the cuckoo.

"How much longer will we be hearing the nightingale's summer song?"

"Around here, all the way through August, and sometimes even into September. From autumn into winter it changes from the sing-song 'ho-hokkekyo' to a harsher 'cha-cha.'"

Kase never tired of hearing the artist talk about nature.

One rainy day in early June Kase took his two students to the nearby big city of Sendai to treat them to a Western meal. The following day he gave them detailed instructions on what to do in his absence. Then he returned to Tokyo for a couple of days.

3

It was just noon when Mizue arrived at the hotel in Shinjuku where she and Kase had last met. He was in the bar drinking Campari and water. She took a seat across the table from him and ordered the same.

"When did you get back?"

"Yesterday afternoon. I haven't been back to Yokohama yet; I spent the night here. Tomorrow afternoon I'll return to Yamagata. How have you been?"

"Fine," said Mizue staring down at the table.

They spent half an hour in the bar, then went to the restaurant for a light lunch before going to Kase's room.

"Is it all right for me to come to your room? It's supposed to be a single room," said Mizue as they were leaving the restaurant.

"I told them there would be two of us today."

The room had twin beds.

"In Yamagata I heard the songs of the nightingale and cuckoo every morning. They always reminded me of the last time we were here. That was the first time I ever felt completely satisfied.," Kase told her.

"I'm glad you feel that way, but there is still a chance that you'll have some regrets later."

"Do you have any hope that things will work out for us in the end?"

Mizue replied that even though she could not join Kase in actually building his gardens, meeting him like this transformed her spiritually and emotionally. "I feel pure and faithful when I'm with you," she said. "What would I do if you didn't believe this and go on believing it for a long time?"

"Do you think I doubt you?"

"Ever since we met last time I've been thinking that if we were just living together, I could have an ordinary life."

"I want you to come live with me, you know that."

"It will never work. I can't just go off and leave my two children."

"Okay, let's not talk about it now." Since they could not know what the future would bring, they should avoid such talk for the time being. Still, it was pleasant for Kase to imagine how Mizue would fit into his simple, physical life. He labored hard during the day, and at night had one drink and went to bed for a sound sleep.

Today, as before, Mizue received Kase into her body and felt transformed.

Mizue left the hotel a bit earlier this time than last. As she was going out of the room, Kase said he would come to Tokyo again if the rainy season this year was a prolonged one.

For several days Mizue was in a state of confusion. She felt now even more strongly than before that she had experienced the full vitality of a creative artist. She could actually feel physical pressure in her breast. This flow of emotions purified her feelings, but it also caused great distress. For the first time, Mizue wondered if real pleasure was always accompanied by pain. And yet when the flow of her emotions had been blocked, she had experienced another sort of pain, one that was physical and emotional. The first time she received Kase into herself, she felt that even this pain intensified. Her confusion now arose from trying to fathom her new feelings of anguish.

Summer had now come to Hadano and to Mizue's garden. One Saturday morning in mid-June Shida said that since tomorrow was Sunday they should all go to Yoshihama to eat seafood.

The children were delighted. There was a restaurant just down the coast at Yoshihama near Yugawara where they sometimes went.

"I don't mind going, but it will be crowded on the highway." Family outings such as this were always hard for Mizue. Whenever they had an outing and she observed other families, it seemed that very few of them were really enjoying themselves. Everyone made a great show of being affectionate to one another, and pretended to be having a good time. To Mizue, they were just phony and showing off.

"The highway only gets crowded in the afternoon. Why don't we leave around ten o'clock and eat lunch there?"

"All right, let's do that."

So it was decided. The next morning they would have a simple breakfast, then travel to the coast at Yoshihama, where they would have shrimp and abalone for lunch. The next morning, however, Mizue's period began two days early. "I can't go like this. I'm sorry to let you down, but can't you just take the children and Momoko and go anyway?"

Her period generally lasted five days and during the whole time Mizue had an uneasy feeling that her menstrual blood gave off an unpleasant odor. She couldn't stand the idea of eating raw seafood.

"The children are looking forward to it, so I guess I'll have to take them," said Shida, but he seemed annoyed that Mizue was not coming. Mizue told the children she could not go because she was not feeling well, but that Momoko would accompany them. The children easily accepted this, because they always enjoyed an outing in the car.

At ten o'clock everyone got in the car and set out, leaving Mizue behind. Since Momoko had already cleaned up the kitchen and done the laundry, Mizue had only to sweep the house. Still, she felt it was a great effort to work at all on the day her period began. She cleaned the bedroom and the children's rooms and then rested.

As she finished cleaning the children's rooms on the second floor, she happened to look down at the garden, and as she did so she heard a flowing sound. It occurred to her that it had rained two days ago and that the Kaneme River was now full. Yesterday afternoon she had looked at the river and seen its muddy water, but what she had just heard was the sound of clear, pure water. She wondered whether this signaled the release of her emotions.

She went downstairs, and then out through the garden to look at the river. It was clear again, and the water only slightly high. At last her confusion was gone, but she thought back to the muddy water yesterday. Her own feelings had cleared like the river. She had told Kase that, living with him, she could become just like any other woman. He had said that was what he hoped for. She wondered if he really felt that way.

It was past three o'clock when the family returned.

"Your husband bought these and asked me to give them to you," said Momoko, presenting her with two abalone and three pieces of fish cake. Mizue felt uncomfortable at seeing the fish cakes, because they had been made by the Kase family's company in Odawara. Still, she had no idea why this upset her.

"Did you go through Odawara?" she asked Momoko, and in her mind she suddenly saw the characters in the company's name.

"No, we bought these at a shop on the road just before the turnoff to Odawara. I believe this is the brand made by Mr. Kase's family."

"I don't feel like eating anything raw today; we'll steam the abalone in saké later."

"I ate all the shrimp and abalone I could. It was a real treat." Momoko thanked Mizue and went to the kitchen with the abalone and fish cakes.

Momoko was a good girl and Mizue hated to let her go, but as Shida had said, they would soon have to find someone for her to marry. All their previous maids had ended up marrying men who worked in Shida's plant.

The men were usually graduates of rural high schools, and after working for seven or eight years they were ready to start families. The company maintained a dormitory for these young workers at nearby Chigasaki, but there was no company housing for married employees. The Shida Ham Company provided the married workers a housing allowance instead.

When the family returned, Shida did not come into the house but went directly to the garage to wash the car, as was his custom every Sunday. Mizue went to their room, and as she entered it she paused in front of the mirror. In the Korean vase beside the mirror was a withered Chinese bellflower. She had just put the flower there that morning. It seemed wrong to have a dead flower beside the mirror, so Mizue took the vase and her scissors and went out into the garden. Here and there were Chinese bellflowers, already in bloom, even though it was only June. Some had bloomed the previous autumn as well.

Mizue cut a single flower and put it in the vase. As she was about to re-enter the home through the back door, she paused to gaze for a moment at her husband as he washed the car. The fish cakes from Kase's family's company were a common item and inexpensive; she often saw them advertised right here in Hadano. Why did the sight of them make her so upset today? Surely, Mizue thought, my good-natured husband has no idea of what is going on. It was just by chance that he bought this brand. Seeing it just makes me feel so unclean.

Mizue had a most unpleasant foreboding. Yet that feeling contained a sense of confidence from having received within herself a man other than her husband. She had never thought her love for Kase would be reflected in this way.

4

The two withered pines beside the artist's house seemed to be reviving; about a month had passed since they had been transplanted. The two students shook their heads in amazement, saying, "I guess the dried cuttle-fish really worked after all."

Kase himself did not really believe the dried cuttlefish had helped. It was obvious the trees had been revived by the fertilizer that had been put on them when they were transplanted. Nevertheless, it was remarkable for a withered pine to recover at all.

Kase wondered if Mizue would be able to purify the crude lust he had been so conscious of the day Emiko called and told him to meet her in Shibuya. He had turned away without entering the hotel where she waited, and had then returned to his office with the same feeling of futility he always felt after sex with her. It was when he came here to Yamagata that the two withered pines had caught his attention. There were plenty of healthy pines around, and his normal response would have been simply to cut the sick ones down. But he happened to recall the passage from the old gardening book—the withered pines seemed emblematic of his own corrupted flesh. Kase wanted to believe in the efficacy of cuttlefish, whether the trees recovered or not.

The newspaper had said there would not be much of a rainy season. The forecast was accurate, and by the end of June the rains still had not come. Kase continued to hear the song of the cuckoo morning and evening. The sound was always muted and distant, the result, the painter said, of the way the bird's song was produced.

Even at the end of June it was still possible to gather tasty wild greens. After school, the children of local farm families would spend their afternoons near the mountain temple, bags of woven straw on their backs, gathering greens in the hills and selling them to earn pocket money. In the orchards in the shallow valley between the temple and the town of Yamagata, the cherries were reaching their full ripeness. Mornings, the breakfast table was positioned in front of the open window so that everyone could hear the birds singing. The old painter could identify many birds just by hearing their songs: "That's woodpecker; there's golden eagle; that one's a shrike; there's a finch."

"It probably took years to learn to tell birds apart like that, just by listening to them," Kase commented one morning.

"Yes, it did. At first I walked around with an illustrated field guide, but that didn't do much good. The best thing was walking around with locals—hunters and people like that. A hunter can catch wild birds very easily using a pole with birdlime on it. When I was just a boy in grammar school there was a hunter in this district called Tomesaku who was very good at catching wild birds. He didn't use a bamboo pole, though. When he went into the mountains, he just took some birdlime with him, and would cut a long, thin, forked branch from a tree. He'd bend down the tip of a branch and smear birdlime on it. I went into the mountains with Tomesaku a number of times and all he had to do was reach that branch up into the air, and before you knew it he'd catch a bird. I don't know how to explain it except that he knew exactly how birds land on tree branches. He even used to catch nightingales that way."

The painter never ran out of interesting stories.

The rains finally came at the beginning of July. According to the weather forecast, intermittent rain would continue for some time, so Kase decided to return to Tokyo with the two students. He would put in the stones once the rainy season ended.

When Kase got to Hodogaya his apartment was stuffy and mildewed. For a time he resumed his normal schedule, commuting back and forth between his place in Hodogaya, his office in Shibuya, and his school in nearby Setagaya. On the eighth day after his return he met Mizue.

As she entered his room at the hotel in Shinjuku, Mizue remarked on how they had already been into the rainy season for quite some time.

"Yes, that's true," said Kase. "But I've been busy with a number of things. Since it will soon be the end of the school term, I've been busy there too. I'm not as pressed as some of those important university professors, but of course I still have to do my job. Anything happen since the last time I was here?"

"Yes and no, It's hard to say, It has more to do with me I guess."

"Oh, really? What do you mean?" Kase turned away from Mizue and looked out the window, thinking it might be better not to ask what's wrong.

"I know I'm being very vague, but it's something that bothers me all the time."

"Is something wrong at home?" At the base of the collar on the outer coat of her kimono was a white splashed pattern against a black background; it dazzled Kase.

"No, everything is in order there, quite uneventful. You probably think I'm upset about giving myself to both you and my husband."

"I hadn't even thought about it. But maybe that's what's bothering you."

"I don't know what I really feel. I'm frightened by the cruelty I see inside myself. But when I'm here with you like this, I feel I've kept all my innocence intact."

"That's too bad for your husband then."

"Tell me what I should do. Help me."

"Come on, you haven't backed yourself into a corner yet."

"Maybe you're right. As I told you, everything is in order, quite uneventful."

"I suppose you still feel attached to your children."

"Are you asking me to leave them and come to you?"

"In the long run that's the only way we can make this work."

"Please don't say that. As a woman I could do it, but as a mother I'd suffer for it, I know I would."

"I understand, but if you leave them, that is the price you'll have to pay."

"It frightens me to hear you say that." Mizue looked directly at Kase. She again felt his words coming to her like the wind blowing among stones on a barren mountain. She'd had an unpleasant premonition the day her husband and children had gone to the coast to eat seafood, but now she felt there was no way to know what the future held, no way to predict what would happen as a result of her affair with Kase.

5

In the Yamagata region there is a kind of lava stone called Yamadera-ishi that is widely used in construction and for building walls. The painter wanted to use this stone for the front wall of his house and had arranged to have local masons come around mid-July, once the rainy season was over. Kase wanted to have the stones for the garden area brought on to the site before the wall was built, so a few days after meeting Mizue at Shinjuku, he went south to Fujinomiya in Shizuoka Prefecture, where there was a quarry with the type of stone he wanted.

He would need a large quantity of rock, since the garden alone was nearly half an acre, larger than any other garden he had made recently. The pine grove on the east side of the house continued beyond the garden and up the side of the mountain. Here he wanted to install a fairly large piece of Fuji stone, one that would stand out against the mountainside when viewed from the house.

Kase had long been acquainted with the old man who ran the Ishihei Stone Company in Fujinomiya, and when Kase arrived there he found him on the veranda of his house eating lunch.

"Well, sir, things aren't going very well just now. Did you know that?" said the man in greeting upon seeing Kase.

"What's wrong?" asked Kase, seating himself on the edge of the veranda.

"You eaten lunch yet?"

"I got a bite to eat at a restaurant near the station."

"It looks like they're going to stop us from quarrying any more Fuji stone here pretty soon."

"Sounds bad. Is it true?"

"I reckon it is. I heard it from a man in the forestry office. Met him in the mountains the other day. I figure it must be true if even the government people are saying it. I guess we've just taken too much stone out of here over the years."

"Tell me, what are your plans over the next few days?"

"I'll be going into the mountains tomorrow and the day after I'll be taking a load of stone to Kamakura, but that's about it for right now."

"How about your son, is he busy?"

"He went to Mie Prefecture for a load of Ise stone. He'll be back tonight, though."

"I'd like you to take a load up to Yamagata for me. I'll be needing a fair amount."

"I think we can handle it."

"Thanks. Go ahead and eat your lunch. I'll be out in the yard checking the stones."

Taking a box of chalk from the veranda, Kase went into the side yard where all the quarried stones had been dumped. There he spread out his design for the painter's garden and once again studied his plan for the placement of the stones. The plans called for twelve large stones, twenty-three-medium sized stones, and thirty small ones. Besides these he needed some two hundred flagstones for the walks. Although any stone can be made to look good if it is placed right, Kase wanted to choose stones whose shapes were appropriate to the garden. For that reason each stone to be individually selected. Holding the plans in one hand, Kase selected the stones, giving special consideration to the slope of the garden and the position of the trees.

Half an hour later, as Kase finished checking off each of the stones he wanted with his white chalk, the old man arrived. The man looked around and counted up the stones that had been marked.

"Besides these I'll need about two hundred stepping stones," Kase told him.

The old man considered for a moment. "I wonder if two trucks will be enough to carry them all." The stones were so heavy, the trucks could not be completely filled.

"Well, you'll manage it somehow, won't you?"

Kase sketched out a rough map for the old man, showing the way from Yamagata City to the mountain temple, and left the stone yard.

He took the train at Fuji City and transferred to the Tokaido Line bound for Tokyo, but he was uncertain exactly where to go. In the end he decided get off en route at Odawara, where his parents lived. It was the first time he had been back for a visit that year.

"You're never home at Hodogaya when I telephone," said Kase's mother when she saw him.

"Why, did something happen?"

"You mean to tell me you won't show up here unless something happens?"

"I'm often out in the countryside. Do you have some fish cakes around? I'm hungry for some."

"Every time you come home, you never say a proper hello, you just ask for fish cakes."

As mother and son talked, Kase's sister-in-law served beer and fish cakes.

"Are you still living alone?" asked his mother after the sister-in-law had left the room.

"Yes, mother. I'm still by myself,"

"Does that mean you don't intend to marry again?"

"Not necessarily. Why?"

His mother told him that the Kiyoda family's daughter, Tamiko, had returned home after her husband died. The Kiyoda family, like Kase's, sold fish cakes. There were about twenty-five households in Odawara that made and sold fish cakes, and since the Kiyodas were related to the Kases, he knew Tamiko. He had heard that she married the second son of a family in Yokohama that operated a large seafood processing company. He learned now from his mother that the previous autumn Tamiko's husband had died of illness, and that in the spring she had returned to her family.

"She has a child, of course, but Tami is only twenty-eight years old. Her parents felt sorry for her and took her back into their home." Kase's mother went on to ask if he wouldn't consider marrying her.

"Don't you think it would be better if she found another businessman to be her second husband?"

After he had drunk the beer and eaten some of the fish cakes to go with it, Kase got to his feet.

"Are you leaving already? Your father will be back from the plant any minute."

"Say hello to him for me."

As Kase left his parents' home and walked toward Odawara Station, he wondered if he should return directly to Hodogaya or go to his office in Shibuya. It was three o'clock on a summer afternoon; it seemed too late to start working, but too early to go home. If he chose to go to Shibuya it would be best to take the express train on the Odakyu Line, but reaching the station Kase bought a ticket for Hodogaya instead.

He had told his mother that Tamiko would be better off marrying another businessman. Kase remembered Tamiko when she was twenty-one or twenty-two. At the time he had been in his early thirties and living alone, just as he was now; he had separated from Emiko and was not yet living with Kazue. It was quite dreary having no women in his life. One spring day he had gone to his parents' house in Odawara for dinner and found Tamiko there. When he saw her, he was startled by her breathtaking freshness. Kase wondered if she had made this impression on him because of his jaded spirit. It had now been five years since he last saw Tamiko. On the train it occurred to him that he might have been interested in Tamiko if he had met her before Mizue.

At Ofuna he transferred to the Yokosuka Line. When he got off at Hodogaya, the oppressive heat of the summer evening assaulted him on all sides. I wonder if I should meet Mizue once more before I go back to Yamagata? Kase's thoughts went back to the hotel in Shinjuku and their last meeting there. She had said that everything was quite in order, but he had sensed a note of desperation in her voice.

6

Mizue felt she was experiencing the full vitality of the landscape architect's creative spirit and there seemed to be no relief for her. She was frightened by the memory of Kase's dispassionate statement that the only solution for her was to abandon her family. Was she beginning to regret her affair with Kase? That did not seem to be the case. She felt that now that her emotions had been unleashed, she would be unable to stop their flow. Mizue had always believed that a happy family will necessarily devise its own routines over time, and she still felt that way. She asked herself if it would be best to think of Kase as someone alien to these family routines. There were a number of simple answers to this, but it was only because they were simple, even simplistic, that they were answers at all. In the end none of them was adequate. Once outside her family, the impediment that kept her emotions locked up within her was gone, and it was in this release that Mizue felt truly cleansed. Hers was not a problem that could be solved by applying conventional moral standards.

One day Ume, the gardener, came. He trimmed the overgrown trees with his shears and the following day pruned the hedge of winter camellia and sasanqua. He also pinched off the fruit that remained after the flowers had fallen, leaving some green fruit that would turn red in autumn as it ripened. There was an especially large amount of fruit on the sasanqua. It was bad to leave too much fruit because it would consume all the shrub's nourishment. When the trees had been pruned, there were spaces opening the garden to the sky that one felt the wind could easily blow in through. Before, the wind seemed only to skip over the tops of the trees, but now it seemed to gust through them.

"Will you be pruning the trees every year?" Mizue asked Ume.

"No. It's not good for the trees to do it every year. They begin to get a shaved look. I only cut the branches when they get too long, every second or third year, depending on the tree."

Ume was pruning the trees according to Kase's instructions. He would not have them cut any old way. One method involved leaving the lower branches alone and clipping the middle branches. There were other techniques too, such as cutting the tops of the trees so they would not grow any taller. In fact, Kase had left specific instructions on how to trim each tree in the Shidas' garden.

After the trees were pruned, areas of the garden that had always been shaded now received scattered sunlight. Mizue found the sunlight beautiful, and when the wind blew, the dappling patterns of light would shift and move in the garden. One afternoon it suddenly occurred to Mizue that it was not that the rays of sunlight moved, but that the branches of the trees were trembling. She was astounded by this observation. She found herself trembling. Kase was shining on her in a steady, unmoving beam, and it was Mizue who was trembling. On days when the wind did not blow, the sunlight did not move either. The shrill cries of the cicadas seemed to pierce the garden, and the sunlight and shadow melted together to become one. Oh, I wish I didn't feel the way I do, thought Mizue. She turned her eyes away from the garden. She was remembering her emotions at the hotel as she opened her body to Kase. She was conscious of the way she would look to the stones in the garden. Even the tree branches were watching her. The garden Kase had built was tying and binding her. Involuntarily she saw the face of her lover saying, "You have no choice but to abandon your family."

71

The calendar said it was the sixteenth of July. It seemed to Mizue that she was checking the date on the calendar far more frequently since she had begun making love to Kase. As she stared at the calendar, she realized her children would soon be out of school for summer vacation. She must meet Kase once again before that happened. Her thirst for him returned. Mizue already knew that her husband could not quench this thirst. With him there was only a physical repetition of the sexual act; there was no fulfillment in it for her. Although Shida had elegant tastes and filled his life with every sort of refined pleasure, he was not a creative person. He understood the arts intellectually, and surrounded himself with artistic things, but his judgments of praise or criticism were only filtered through the eyes of a dilettante.

On the afternoon of July eighteenth, there was a telephone call from Kase.

The following afternoon Mizue met Kase at the hotel in Shinjuku and talked with him about the patterns of sunlight in the garden.

Kase asked if she felt that she was the only one who shook and trembled.

"But isn't it true you're watching me every day through the garden?"

"I wonder. Once it's aroused your feelings, it should become just an ordinary garden."

"Do you really think so?"

Mizue knew that Kase was right. Although the garden had originally been the objective, Kase believed that its outward appearance should have changed for Mizue now that she had had direct emotional contact with the artist who made it. Kase did not like to always boast about the gardens he had built; it was enough that their worth was recognized.

"Last time you said your family life was quiet and uneventful. Is it still that way?" Kase asked.

"Things are the same for me as a wife. But as a woman, they're far from boring and tranquil."

"It must be hard for you."

"How long will you be in Yamagata this time?"

"A month. It will take that long to get the stones set in place."

"And during that time will you . . . ?"

"No, I won't be able to come back until the garden is finished."

"While the children have their summer holiday I won't be able to leave home anyway. I'll expect to hear from you in September. Is it all right if I ask you a very personal question?"

"What is it?

"Do you plan to go for such a long time without seeing a woman?"

"I'm used to it. One month is not such a long time. Sometimes I have dreams though."

"What did you do before you had me?"

"My first wife came to visit sometimes at Hodogaya, but I've broken off with her since I've been seeing you."

"Thank you."

Mizue felt sorry, however, that she had asked that question. She felt it rather unbecoming and was irritated with herself.

While making love to Kase, Mizue saw clearly in her mind the shape of the garden. In a soft voice she murmured, "Let yourself go, don't hold back. It will be more than a month before we see each other again." Since she could not know what lay in store for them, she accepted Kase within herself and again felt transformed. This was nothing more than an inward returning to herself. It was the only thing she could do.

7

With the end of the rainy season, summer was at its height in Yamagata. It was considerably cooler around the mountain temple than in Yamagata City. Kase was accompanied by the same two students who had been with him in June. After lunch they would spend an hour resting in the shade of a tree. It was heavy work getting the stones set. They had the help of the three local gardeners and every day all six of them would work at moving the stones into place. The largest stones were hoisted with a crane mounted on a truck, but it still took a great deal of work before they got the stone set as they wanted it.

Fair weather continued, and peaches were ripening in the nearby orchards. The painter or his wife often sent one of the maids out to buy some. These peaches were then chilled in the well and served firm, almost crisp. "I don't care much for those soft peaches that you see in the stores today. I always have them get this kind," the painter said.

The skins of these peaches were still green, and they were tart when you bit into them.

Kase agreed with the painter. "You're exactly right. There is something very natural about these peaches."

"The same goes for apples," said the painter. "If they're not crisp, they just won't do." Such talk continued—the grapes would soon be ready, by mid-August they would be eating green apples, and so on.

In the mornings, just as before, they could hear the distant cry of the cuckoo. The bird song made Kase acutely aware of where he was, at the foot of a mountain. He observed the painter's daily life. It seemed completely wholesome, with nothing to disturb his peace of mind.

"You've spent all your life painting. Was there ever a time when it seemed to you that your art would destroy you?" Kase asked the painter one morning at breakfast.

"Hmmm. I'm not sure. My paintings have always been the most commonplace sort, and I guess that even if there was such a period in my career, I must have passed through it without realizing it."

Kase decided the painter was just being modest.

"Why do you ask?" said the painter. "Are you troubled about your own career?"

"No, I'm not troubled now, though I was at one time. But one thing still bothers me. Even if I build a garden I think is just fine, I am always afraid people who see it will think it lacks sophistication and depth." Kase mentioned this because of what Mizue had said about her garden the last time he had seen her. Kase had told her that if the garden could arouse her feelings, it would become just an ordinary garden. But if Mizue still felt she was being watched by the garden now that they were lovers, it was an indication he had created something raw and unrefined.

"I think you worry too much about it. As far as I can see you've really made quite a good garden here, though one does have to be alert to appreciate its finer points. I've been watching you for some time now while you've been placing the stones, and I think the garden will be quite natural looking. Have you seen many of the temple gardens in Kyoto?"

"Yes. I've seen them all. It's part of my job."

"Do you feel that any of them lack sophistication and depth?"

"I feel that way about the abbot's garden at the Tofukuji, where you have a tall rock composition and then a checkerboard pattern of flat stones and bushes."

"Oh, really? I believe you're right, that garden is rather crude. But isn't it just that it hasn't aged long enough? After all, it's barely thirty years old."

"You're right about its age, but I wonder if it will really lose that shallowness over time. The man who built it was the best garden designer of his generation, but it's as if the garden is too human. Every garden that man built seems to generate a kind of hot passion."

"That is the feeling you get. But when you consider how it will look two hundred years from now, your perspective on it changes, doesn't it?"

There was something to this comment. Kase did not have a deep understanding of Zen and consequently he tended to avoid Zen rock gardens. He would remember what the painter said.

They finished placing the stones right on schedule around the middle of August. Both the stepping stones that led down to the river and the ones that led through the grove of red pines achieved a nice effect. After that Kase and his crew spent four days working with local gardeners to put in the lawn. Then they spread fertilizer on it and the garden was completed.

"It's a lovely garden." The painter seemed especially pleased that, from the house, the river could be seen through the trees. From the garden, the land sloped gently down to the river, so no steps were required. Thinking there might be a problem if the river flooded, Kase had rolled boulders down along the edge of the water and behind them buried a row of granite stones. The placing of stones throughout the pine grove along the east side of the house had also turned out well. The garden was very naturalistic. The design seemed artless, yet it distilled nature.

"Replace the hemp ropes about this time next year. The rope eats into the growing tree." Kase left this and other instructions for the local gardener.

75

The painter urged Kase to take several days of well-earned rest at a nearby hot springs resort, but Kase said he didn't feel like it just then. He left Yamagata the next morning. The two students returned by car.

Kase went first to his office in Shibuya, where his staff briefed him on what had happened during his absence. Late that night he returned to his apartment.

He planned to spend the rest of August vacationing, and the next afternoon he set out for his family's home in Odawara. He had only one project in Tokyo lined up for the fall. The house itself was just being built, so he would have to wait until it was finished. The client for this garden was a conservative politician. Kase was not particularly interested in doing this job. He would go see the house as soon as it was completed and if it was too rich and tasteless, he intended to refuse the job.

"I'll only be here to bother you for a couple of weeks," said Kase as he entered his parents' house.

"There'll be a blue moon tonight," laughed his mother, surprised to see her son return home.

"I just need a rest," he said. "Really all I need is beer and fish cakes. I don't want to trouble you too much."

"You're always making trouble around here!" Kase's mother was in fact delighted that he was going to stay for two weeks.

8

By mid-August, Mizue realized she was behaving strangely. In July she had asked Kase to call her in September, but there was really no reason for such an arrangement. After all, she could still get away to go to Shinjuku, even if the children were home from school. Her regret for having suggested waiting so long surfaced as soon as she began to feel a thirst for Kase's love. Nothing had changed between her and her husband; they were getting along well enough together, and yet her desire did not displease her.

Throughout the month this craving had grown. It was not just sex with

Kase that was needed to restore her emotional balance; apparently there was something in Kase himself that gave Mizue a sense of wholeness. Having sex might slake her thirst, but she also felt it would be enough if she could just see and talk to Kase.

Mizue continued to feel that the garden was watching her. Some days she would walk through it and down to the river. Even though she knew precisely where each stone was located, when she passed through the trees she would suddenly, unexpectedly encounter a stone and be startled. The stones did not exactly stare at her, but she felt she was being watched by them. The trees had their seasons, when the color of their leaves changed and intensified, but the stones remained unchanging. Mizue had watched when the stones had first been set in place. About two-thirds of each stone was sunk in the ground with only the remaining third visible. Whenever she felt she was being watched by the stones in the garden, she became uncertain about how deeply each one was really buried.

When her thirst for love reached its peak, she felt she would lose her mind, but there was nothing she could do about it.

One night Mizue and her husband made love. The next morning, when Shida had gone to work, the children were upstairs reading, and Momoko was doing the laundry, Mizue decided to call Kase's office in Shibuya. She learned that he was in Odawara, and called there right away. A woman answered but a moment later Kase came on the line.

"I want to see you," she declared.

"Today?"

"Yes."

"Can you come right now?"

"Yes."

"All right. I'll be waiting for you around eleven o'clock at the main gate of Odawara Station."

Mizue immediately got ready to go out. She wore a white linen kimono with a scattered black pattern.

Having dressed, she told Momoko she would be out until around three o'clock and left. On the train to Odawara she kept thinking it was crazy to be doing this. She had been physically satisfied during the night, so it was not a matter of needing sex. And yet, she still had this thirst for love.

Arriving at Odawara she went out the main gate to where Kase was waiting.

"I'm sorry to bother you. I'm afraid I'm being very selfish."

"Oh no, not at all. It's quite all right with me. There are no suitable places around here, so I called and reserved a room up at one of the hot spring resort hotels at Hakone."

They got a taxi in front of the station, but traffic was heavy, and it was almost an hour before they reached the hotel.

It was an old wooden building. The maid who showed them to their room told them the place was filled with people who had come to the mountains to escape the heat. All that was vacant was a room on the first floor that did not have a very good view.

Mizue did not care whether they had a view or not.

"It certainly is cool here," remarked Kase. A breeze was coming in the window.

Mizue changed into one of the hotel's lightweight yukata robes and went to the bath. It was deserted, and she stayed only a moment to wash the perspiration from her body. When she returned to the room, Kase was drinking beer.

"I wonder how high above sea level we are here?"

"I don't know for sure, but I suppose it must be more than two thousand feet. Anyway, it's cool."

When Kase finished his beer he went to the bath to wash. "I don't care much for hot springs resorts. I can't understand those people who spend several days at one and do nothing but go to the bath several times a day."

"Other people are other people; you are you."

"You're right, of course. Today you're acting like you really feel desperate. I noticed it as soon as I saw you at Odawara." Kase picked up the phone and ordered saké and several dishes of food.

Mizue spoke to him of her inner thirst. Kase thought it was simply a matter of self-indulgence. It was insane, this bond that existed now between them. A person who could not find complete self-fulfillment would always be plagued by a burning thirst. Kase felt the same way himself.

Mizue told him that she had had sex with her husband the previous night, and the fact that she was still unable to feel satisfied had nothing to do with mere sex.

The food and saké they ordered arrived. Kase began to feel warm as he drank. "So how do you propose to quench this thirst of yours?"

"I don't know. The only thing I know is that I have to see you more often."

"It's warm. I'm going to take my clothes off." Kase opened his yukata at the chest and pulled it back over his shoulders, exposing the upper half of his body.

Mizue joined him in drinking a little saké.

"You know, it's really dangerous for us to be meeting at a place like this. Shida Ham sells its products throughout this entire region. But if you are determined that we be together, I guess it doesn't really matter."

"What would you do if I do decide that's what I want?"

"Naturally I'll tell your husband our relationship is completely satisfying."

"You couldn't possibly. Besides, it would be too hard on my children. It's completely out of the question." Mizue paused. "When did you get back from Yamagata?"

"Today is my third day in Odawara. I got back from Yamagata the day before that."

"Have you been without a woman all this time? I'm sorry, it's rude of me to ask that."

"It's just as I told you it would be."

"That's all right then. I want to feel you inside me."

Kase rose to his feet and closed the paper screens that opened on the garden, then seated himself next to Mizue. "Let me see you," he said, putting his hand inside her yukata.

A moment later they were lying side by side on the mats. Mizue closed her eyes.

Kase opened her yukata. To him, her thirty-three-year-old body was more than an object to be looked at. She was more than a mere receptacle; she was an object of serene contemplation. How long, Kase wondered, could they fulfill each other so completely? He gazed at her sleek body, neither too fat nor too thin, the body of another man's wife. She had given birth to two children, but her lower belly was still tight and lovely. Emiko's belly was scarred by lateral stretch marks and dark spots. Kase had heard that these blemishes occur when a woman gives birth to a large child.

Kase placed the palm of his right hand on Mizue's pubic mound and with his left hand spread her thighs.

THE GARDEN PATH

(The Garden at Konchi-in)

1

There is an old book called *Roji Kikigaki*, or "Accounts of the Garden Path," that describes the construction of tea gardens. It is not clear who its author was, but judging from the literary style of the text Kase guessed it was probably a work of the Edo period. Apparently it had been written as a result of the author's reading of the *Nanporoku*—"Southern Chronicles"—and various other works dealing with detached tea houses. It was not an innovative work, but it did gather together a number of techniques for building tea gardens—including path construction, stepping stones, stones for the entry door, stones for the middle gate, stone lanterns, placement of the wash basin stone, and ornamental stones—and thus was an important reference for any landscape architect. It was from this book that Kase learned the method of arranging garden stones. There is no better way to position stones than the techniques it describes for winding paths and for stones in clusters of three or five. Ultimately, however, it was nothing more than a reference tool. Kase had to be careful. Even with the help of such a book, it was still possible to make a tea garden that seemed artificial, like a bonsai. When a tea garden is too elaborate, it becomes contrived, and those who know gardens can't bear to look at it.

The conservative politician in Tokyo who had asked Kase to build a nice Japanese-style garden had just completed building his house. Kase went to inspect the site.

"I'll think about it," said Kase as he left the house.

He returned to his office in Shibuya and wrote the politician a letter declining to design a garden for him, saying that such a project was beyond his ability. The house itself was a mixture of Japanese and Western styles, and in the living room hung a gaudy, tasteless chandelier. The politician boasted that the chandelier had been imported from Italy.

Three days later the politician's private secretary appeared at Kase's office in Shibuya. "You are being too modest when you say you can't handle a job like this," said the secretary. "We want you to start work right away."

Kase replied bluntly. "The house is in bad taste. Any garden I built would not be appropriate there."

The secretary glared at Kase. "Oh, I see," he sputtered, and stalked out of the office.

The politician's house violated good taste in several respects. It has been a common practice since the late nineteenth century for an ordinary Japanese-style house to have one or two Western rooms in it. But to provide that room with a bright red carpet and a crystal chandelier was going too far. Even hotel rooms aren't decorated that way these days. The whole house had a rococo feel about it, and there was no reason to suppose that a Japanese-style garden would harmonize with it. Kase told the politician's secretary that instead they ought to put in a garden that had palm trees, fountains, and pools. He hated to see anyone casually abuse and ignore traditional concepts of beauty. The politician was building a detached tea house in his garden and had wanted Kase to design a garden path and tea garden for him, but Kase could not see how it was possible to artistically link the gaudy main house with a plain style tea house. Nor could he imagine the spiritual and emotional resources of a man who would undertake such a project. Kase was afraid that if he built a garden in front of the tea house, it would seem artificial and out of harmony with the main house, which was physically connected to the tea house by an open corridor. Had the two buildings been completely separated, Kase might have been willing to put in an independent garden path.

At the hotel at Hakone, as soon as Kase had laid Mizue down, he had realized how emblematic she was of both the path and the garden it penetrated. The method of placing stones set forth in "Accounts of the Garden Path" had shades of meaning not to be understood by a young gardener who had never known a woman. Take, for example, the placing of the stepping stones for a path. Even though the stones are placed irregularly in what appears to be a disorderly manner, they nevertheless follow a single, direct line. According to the diagrams in the book, each step was formed by a cluster of seven stones. On the right five large stones are arranged to form a crook, and on the left are two small stones. The two small stones and the five large ones worked together to make a single cluster. The other possible combination would be a cluster of three stones, with two large stones and a small one. The arrangements could be achieved effortlessly, and if they were not convenient for walking, they were nevertheless appealing in appearance.

One evening late in autumn, after he had completed such a path, Kase walked along it, stepping on the large stones: right, left, right, left. This arrangement of stones reminded him of the mature woman's body. Perhaps anything overly assertive reminded him of such a woman. Still, this garden itself was not unrefined. If the stones were poorly arranged, the garden would have a crude feeling about it, but this could be redeemed by the placement of the surrounding trees.

One year Kase had run off to Kyoto in the middle of August to visit the abbot's garden at the Tofukuji temple. On that occasion the garden had struck him as unrefined. This did not mean, of course, that the stones had been placed unskillfully; indeed, their placement was flawless. The man who had made this garden was considered the best garden designer of his time—he had lived only a single generation before Kase. Kase wondered what his spiritual and emotional condition had been when he built it. It was odd that the garden had an aura of superficiality, since at the same time it was quite forbidding. The entrance and garden of a fine restaurant would be far more casual than this, and yet, oddly enough, the restaurant garden would not seem crude. The garden at Tofukuji lacked profundity even though it was composed entirely of stones and sand. Kase suspected that when the garden had been built, the designer had been unable to filter out his ego. It was always possible, of course, that Kase was wrong about this; and besides, he had nothing with which to substantiate his doubts.

2

At the hotel at Hakone Kase had said, "Let me see you," and had suddenly clutched Mizue's breast with his hand. At that moment Mizue felt that some vital part of her was being taken from her. It was a feeling she had never known before. Just as she felt she might faint, Kase told her how he had realized her body was like the path in a tea garden.

"What do you mean?" asked Mizue when her mind had cleared a little.

"I mean the stepping stones of the garden path. In order to proceed along the path you have to step first to the right and then to the left, but you are always moving forward in a direct line. I have a feeling somehow that the gardens I build from now on will be shallow."

"Will that be because you've known me?"

"Yes."

"Are you sorry this happened?"

"No. Not at all. I'm grateful to you."

"Why does everything seem so confusing when I'm with you?"

Mizue dozed on the train returning to Hadano. She missed her station and, awakening at Isehara, scrambled off the train and caught a taxi home. Until her husband returned that evening, she spent the rest of the day in a daze, uncertain whether she was awake or dreaming.

By early September Mizue was meeting Kase about once a week. Each time she set out for the rendezvous, Mizue felt she was acting impulsively, out of physical desire. When she surrendered her body to Kase, she felt removed from herself, as though seeing herself from the outside.

One day toward the end of September she spent the day with Kase and returned home. At dinner she was aware that Kase had watched her with a certain kind of look, and that she was now observing her husband the same way. It was an odd sensation. But somehow before she was quite aware of it, she realized the sensation was growing within her. While she felt happy that the flow of her emotions had begun, she also felt she had behaved disgracefully. Mizue realized there had not been a single day since Kase appeared that her feelings and emotions had been normal. Physically she felt satisfied, but at the same time, her heart ached. Her emotions were in conflict.

That night as Mizue went to bed, her husband said, "You seem to be going out quite a lot recently."

"Would you rather I didn't?" Mizue was caught off guard, but managed to answer calmly.

85

"It's not that I mind. I just wonder why you've been going out so often."

When she heard her husband speak to her like this, Mizue felt rebellion well up within her. Neither husband nor wife said anything more and retired to their separate beds.

Alone in her own bed, Mizue wondered what she would do if her husband found out. She had tried to believe Kase when he said he could prove that their affair was completely fulfilling for both of them, but she felt sorry for the children. Ashamed, Mizue finally fell asleep.

The next morning when she got up and began to dress, her husband said, "Please try to keep from going out so often." Mizue felt a sudden stab of fright at this comment: Shida was usually still asleep at this hour. She looked at him and saw that his eyes were still closed. Her mind went back to the time she had spent with Kase at the hotel in Hakone. She remembered him saying it was dangerous to meet in such a place. Mizue again felt ashamed and left the bedroom without a word in reply.

3

Early in September Eiji Shida stopped by the company's headquarters in Fujisawa. While he was there his father, Sakuzo, asked if he was keeping a close eye on his wife.

"What do you mean?" asked Shida.

"I hope I'm mistaken," said his father.

Sakuzo Shida had taken a holiday at the end of August. He explained that he and his wife had gone to Hakone, where they had spent three days at a hotel. The second afternoon he had happened to glance down from the mezzanine toward the hotel entrance. He watched a man and a woman get into a taxi. The woman looked like Mizue. He only saw her from behind, and since tree branches obscured the view he could not be certain it was her, but the woman's figure resembled Mizue's very closely.

"She was wearing a white linen kimono. Right away I tried calling your home. Momoko answered and said Mizue was out. I spoke to one of the maids in the hotel and asked who the departing couple were, but she said she did not know. Then I spoke to the desk clerk. He said he did not know who the woman was, but the man had connections with a fish cake business in Odawara. How do you explain that?"

"I can't. You must be mistaken." Yet even as he spoke, Shida recalled the face of Yusaku Kase. It was unbelievable.

"If I am mistaken about this, I owe you an apology."

"You're mistaken," said Shida, but he knew his father was right. Sakuzo was not the sort of father who would casually say something that could destroy his son's family. And yet it was unbelievable. Instead of feeling outrage or anguish, Shida could only wonder, Why? He had always been told by his parents and brother that he was too easygoing. Yet other people had always praised his competence in looking after his own affairs. He had always relied on the fact that he possessed these qualities. It simply had never occurred to him that his wife might be unfaithful.

From that day on Shida observed his wife from a new perspective. She appeared unchanged, and yet his feelings about her had changed. There was nothing he could do for comfort except increase the amount of time he spent on the tea ceremony or in listening to music. Mizue's infidelity was completely unreal, completely separated from anything Shida had ever experienced. He consoled himself, however, with the thought that there was no real proof of adultery. Still, he was afraid, wondering if and when this last refuge of uncertainty would be lost.

4

Early in October when she met Kase at their usual hotel in Shinjuku, Mizue told him she thought her husband suspected something.

"What do you plan to do about it?" asked Kase.

"I don't know."

"Does he know that I am your lover?"

"He's the sort of person who doesn't show much on the surface." Mizue said, "So I just don't know how much he knows."

"Why don't you talk to him about it?"

"I can't."

"But since he has some suspicions, we can't go on meeting secretly like this," Kase said.

"What would I accomplish by talking to him?"

"I want you to come and live with me."

"I can't do that. It would be too sad for the children."

"But since he suspects something, we can't keep on this way."

"I don't know what to do. Now that things have reached this point, I just don't know what to do. You're probably laughing at me for being so silly."

"Of course not," Kase told her. "I don't think there is anything funny about it at all. But the problem has a cause, so there must also be a solution. Everyone has both an instinct for life and an instinct for death. In your case, it would have made no difference if your lover had been someone else. For you the problem is not simply one of infidelity or sexual desire. Remember in June when you went to visit the cemetery at Oiso and we met?"

"Yes. It was June of last year."

"I remember you told me you had lost three members of your family within half a year."

"Yes," Mizue said. "My father died in June, mother in September, and my brother in December."

"I imagine at that time you felt as though you wanted to die too. You must have had that feeling even if you weren't conscious of it. Up until the time you met me, you must have felt something; if it was not exactly an instinct for death, then perhaps a death wish. Then you met me, things turned out the way they did, and your death wish went away. I began to interpret our affair this way that afternoon at Hakone, when you told me you had a thirst. If your husband is suspicious, sooner or later we'll have to deal with things."

"I said I thought he was becoming suspicious, but all he said was he didn't like me going out so often, so perhaps there is nothing to worry about after all."

"No. I don't think so. Somehow he has come pretty close to guessing the truth. That's how I feel anyway."

"I don't like to hear you say things like this."

Since that afternoon in Hakone, Mizue felt that every time she gave her body to Kase, some vital part of her was being whittled away. Today she felt the same way. Previously her craving had only taken the form of psychological stagnation, but ever since Hakone her physical desire had consumed her whenever she was unable to meet Kase. Each time she surrendered her body to him she attained a feeling of ecstasy and self-forgetfulness. When she returned to her senses, however, she realized she would have to bear the consequences of these feelings. It was clear to Mizue that she could view herself objectively. Today the feeling that some vital part of her had been diminished was stronger than ever, perhaps because she felt Shida suspected what was going on. Her sense of her own dissoluteness caused friction between herself and her complacent husband. And so she exhausted herself by subjecting her body completely to Kase.

She returned home shortly before four. Shida was washing the car. Mizue had a premonition of trouble when she saw this, for her husband never came home before six o'clock.

That evening Shida confronted her.

"My father saw you on the afternoon of August twenty-seventh. You left the hotel at Hakone with a man and got into a taxi. I tried not to believe it. I tried to persuade myself it was not absolutely certain. I told my father he must have been mistaken. But he wasn't. I knew you were going out again today. I could tell by the way you acted. I followed you. I saw you two in the hotel lobby and I came home after that. Why did you want to destroy our family?"

"Please don't get so upset." Listening to her husband, Mizue regained her own composure.

"I am upset. You don't understand what you're doing; not at all. Why did you destroy our family? I want to hear the reason."

"I don't believe I destroyed our family, although I guess you feel it has been ruined. I just needed to be with someone."

"I can't believe that."

"I feel the same way; I can't believe it either. But it's true. I needed love."

"How long has this been going on?"

"Since May. If you want to hit me, I won't try to stop you. I have no excuses for what I have done."

"If I wanted to hit you, I would have done it before this. When I left the hotel lobby, I came straight back here. I've washed the car twice. I didn't know what else to do. I thought about the children. Am I really the considerate sort of person people say I am, or am I just a fool? Probably a fool. What do you intend to do now? Haven't you even considered what this means for the children?"

"I don't know what to do now. Of course I've thought about the children. And right now I feel that what I have done must be terrible for you. But I couldn't help it. It didn't have to be Kase. It's true I needed love, but somewhere deep within myself I felt there was no reason for me to live. I've felt this way ever since my father, mother, and brother died. Kase said I should tell you everything. I guess I probably should have told you sooner."

"Do you plan to desert your family and go live with him? Have you promised him something like that?"

"No I have to think of the children. Kase said I would have to give up the children, but I just can't bring myself to do that."

"Damn that gardener! What a bastard." This outburst was accompanied by a slap across the face that turned Mizue's head. Shida stalked out of the bedroom and returned shortly with a bottle of brandy and two glasses. He poured brandy into the glasses and placed one in front of Mizue. "Drink!" he ordered.

Shida drained his brandy at a single gulp and said, "I feel like going crazy. Don't worry, I won't hit you again, but drink that."

"I can't drink that, it's too strong."

"What do you mean? Think of what you've made me swallow. Compared to that this is nothing. Drink it!"

"Try to calm down. The children or Momoko will hear us."

"You mean you're ashamed of this mess and you want to hide it?"

Mizue knew Shida was normally soft-spoken and considerate of others, even Momoko.

"Eiichi is ten, Noriko is eight, your husband is thirty-seven, and you, thirty-three; what did you find wrong with our family? If you felt there was no reason to go on living, why didn't you die sooner? What you're saying now is just an excuse."

"Yes. Perhaps you are right."

"Drink that!"

Mizue sipped the brandy.

"If you wanted to destroy our family, you should have done it before we made it. You don't know what you have done to me. Tomorrow I will destroy the garden. And not just the garden, everything. Drink!"

Shida kept muttering, "That son of bitch."

Mizue's glass was still half full. Normally her consumption of alcohol was limited to a glass of beer or two small sips of saké. She did not think she could drink all the brandy, but felt she would have to.

The next thing she knew, Shida had stripped off her clothes. "Let's see you drink it naked. You and I have been intimate enough, you can do it." Mizue knew her husband was not merely being perverse.

"You sit there naked and think back over all the things we've done together. What do you mean when you say you have no reason to go on living? Don't be so selfish. It is better to die than make excuses. If you had gone off and committed suicide with that son of a bitch gardener, I might have understood. But no, you couldn't do that, you had to go to a hotel and commit your filthy acts. Listen to me! No matter how upset I get, at least I am still decent and clean. Don't forget that."

The brandy bottle was already two-thirds empty and Mizue was so dizzy she could no longer sit upright. "I have the power now to make you live or let you die," said Shida.

Oddly enough, when her husband entered her, Mizue felt she was being assaulted, and found it pleasurable. Never before had it been like this when her husband made love to her. She opened herself to him like a criminal and gave herself up to the flow of sensation. Even with her head reeling from drunkenness, she was conscious of each thrust.

The next morning she found herself lying naked in bed. Shida's bed was empty. She looked at the bedside clock, and saw it was past ten. She thought back over the grotesque events of the previous day. She could not endure it. She had thought some vital part of her was being whittled away, and once that was gone, her body itself would deteriorate; she felt she would be physically destroyed.

Mizue got up and went into the family room. Momoko was there. "Your husband said you have a cold and told me to see that you stay in bed today."

"Thank you. Did the children get off to school all right?"

"Yes. Would you like some breakfast, ma'am?"

"Not right now, but I would like a glass of water."

Mizue drank the water, then ate three tangerines and went back to bed. Her hips and thighs felt numb. She was unable to get up. Men are terrible, she thought. She did not have the strength to move.

When she awoke again, it was nearly two in the afternoon. She washed her face and sat down in front of the mirror. There she saw reflected the events of the previous day. She felt fortunate; Shida could have done far worse than leave her body feeling numb. Her husband was more mature than she had realized.

When she finished making up her face, she ate three more tangerines, then made a phone call to Kase's office in Shibuya. The receptionist answered and said that Kase was expecting a guest and had returned to Hodogaya. Mizue thought the guest was probably her husband. If his guest had come on business, it would not have been necessary to meet in Hodogaya. She called Kase's apartment.

He answered the phone. "Is he there now?" asked Mizue.

"Yes, he's here."

"We had a terrible scene last night. He's a businessman and usually knows how to keep his composure. But I'm afraid that there will be difficulties if you don't take me in."

"I understand, I . . . "

Kase broke off in mid-sentence and her husband's voice came on the line, "Why are you calling him here?"

"Well, everything is in the open now. You know how you behaved last night. It was terrible."

"Are you suggesting that all this is may fault?" He hung up the phone.

5

It was ten-thirty in the morning and Kase was at his office in Shibuya when the phone call came from Eiji Shida. Shida said he wanted to talk about Mizue. Kase recalled the previous day when Mizue had said she thought her husband was suspicious. He asked Shida to meet him at his home in Hodogaya at two o'clock. It would be impossible for them to talk at his office or at a coffee shop.

Shida appeared precisely at two o'clock. "Has Mizue ever come here?" he asked as he entered the room.

"Never."

"Then you've usually met at that hotel in Shinjuku?"

"That's right."

"Why have you done this?"

"Why? There's no reason why. Look, Shida, you've seen what's happened. It's all out in the open. This is not something you can solve by looking for causes or reasons. Why don't you just calm down and let Mizue come and live with me."

"The problem is not quite as simple as that."

At this point the phone call came from Mizue.

"Look, Shida," said Kase,"can't we settle this in a businesslike way?"

"If it was a car accident or something like that we could settle it in a businesslike way. I don't want Mizue to leave me. Everyone makes mistakes sometimes. If a person lets his injuries get exaggerated out of proportion every time he gets hurt, he could not go on living. What exactly do you have in mind when you say we should settle this in a businesslike way?"

"I want you to allow Mizue to come and live with me."

"Listen, Kase, you're talking to me like we're equals in this."

"Aren't we?"

"That's not the point. When you speak of settling this in a businesslike way, you mean a divorce. Well, you know all about divorce. You've been through two of them. But you're wrong if you think I will give Mizue a divorce. I intend to take her back and cure her. I want her to stop seeing you."

"What if she can't be cured?"

"Now listen to me, Kase. I'm a businessman and I pride myself on being able to control my temper, but I'll tell you this, you're pushing me now."

Kase could see that Shida was straining to keep his temper. "All right, so I've been divorced twice. Each time it was partly my fault. I'll admit that.

But you have to understand that with Mizue I'll be different. It's hard to explain what I mean, but I'll be different."

"If I let her come to you, you'd just end up being divorced a third time. I plan to take her back and make her see that she's made a mistake. I don't care what it takes. I don't ever want you to see my wife again. I want you to promise me that."

Sometime after that Shida left. Kase telephoned Mizue and told her the gist of the conversation.

"It's not going to work. I have my children to think of. Please give me some time to think it over," said Mizue.

"You said you had a terrible scene last night. Did he beat you?"

"He only hit me once. It was not like what you imagine."

"I suppose we won't be able to see each other for a while?"

"No. Somehow I'll manage to see you, but please understand, it will take a little time."

After he hung up, Kase decided that given Mizue's attachment to her children, it was not going to be easy to persuade her to leave them. Neither moral persuasion nor an appeal to her conscience would work. In any case, Kase was grateful that Shida had acted so restrained in all this.

Kase felt his relationship with Mizue had not fulfilled its potential. He had never had any illusions about how things stood. He moved forward only when some object or some woman motivated him. He always acted on his own, aloof from the conventions of society. Building gardens, of course, was a job that encouraged this autonomy.

Still, no matter what Shida said, Kase realized that Mizue was now an essential part of his life. It was through Mizue that for the first time he had found fulfillment. Kase felt in the depths of his being that the completeness of his experience with her remained unchanged. Whenever she was with him, he felt vitally alive.

At that moment Kase believed that Shida's presence was intolerable. It was a fact that Mizue had a husband and children, but Kase felt that Mizue must have freed herself from them. Otherwise, she could not have let her body give itself so completely to him. Kase did not feel that his affair with Mizue was everything it could be, but he was aware of its potential. In Mizue's sleek body, with its rich skin, he saw a well-made tea garden path.

One could not enter the tea house unless one trod the path. Just walking the path itself was a source of joy.

6

After learning of the affair between Mizue and Kase, Eiji Shida rarely put in an appearance at the company's headquarters at Fujisawa. The Atsugi plant produced ham, sausage, and bacon, while the Hiratsuka plant turned out canned hams. Most days, Shida went to the Atsugi plant and immersed himself in his work. Two years before they had installed a sausage-making machine and a smoker purchased from Swiss and German manufacturers. The Shida Ham plant boasted the most modern equipment, but still smoked with natural firewood—although it would have been easy to use the German smoking machine—because many customers still preferred the natural smoke flavor. These specially smoked hams and bacons were generally produced at Atsugi because of the unlimited supply of beech wood from the nearby Tanzawa mountains.

The brick smokehouse at the Atsugi plant was a relic from the early days of the Shida Ham Company. Nowadays it was called a smokehouse, but when Shida was a child, it had been referred to as the smoker.

Today Shida was at the smokehouse checking on the latest batch of bacon. Countless hooks with fat slabs of pork impaled on them hung from the ceiling. After it had been smoked for a day and a night with a smoldering fire of beech chips, the bacon would be completely cured and have a rich color. Shida also smoked salmon and other meats for his own family's use.

In its line of hams the Shidas' company produced hams with bones, boneless hams, roast ham, and pressed ham; recently it had begun making a sandwich ham as well. Its sausages included linked, smoked, patties, frankfurters, Vienna, and salami. As society became more complex and lifestyles more elaborate, the meat processing industry also produced a greater variety of products.

"Hello. Are you in there?" the voice came from the door of the smoker.

Shida turned to find his plant foreman standing there.

"We've got a good unit of bacon here," said Shida, turning the rest of the job over to one of the workmen as he left the smokehouse.

"There's a man named Kase here to see you."

Shida felt a surge of bitterness. What's that bastard doing here? he wondered. Kase was already waiting for him in the reception room.

Shida washed his hands, took off his protective work jacket, and went into the reception room.

"I'm sorry to bother you like this," said Kase. "I know you must be busy."

"What are you doing here?" asked Shida.

"I've been in Atsugi buying trees and am just on my way home. I was afraid I might bother you, but I dropped in anyway. Do you really have to have her?"

"Did you come all the way here just to talk about that?"

"I haven't seen Mizue since the last time I talked to you. So I want to talk to you again and work something out."

"What do you mean, work something out? You've already ruined my wife and the mother of my two children. How can you talk about working something out? I'm really not interested in whatever solutions you would care to propose. I thought I told you last time that I do not want you to see my wife ever again. You promised me that."

"We're both grown men. Can't we talk about this like adults?"

"You haven't behaved in a very mature way."

"I see. If that's the way you feel about it, then I guess there's nothing left to discuss. Goodbye." Kase left without even taking a sip of his tea.

That miserable bastard, thought Shida, staring at the seat Kase had occupied. He really has some nerve.

That evening Shida told his wife that Kase had visited him at the plant at Atsugi. "He told me that since we are both grown men, we should talk about this like adults. I thought I'd feel better once I made you realize your mistake. I kept reminding myself that no one can go on living if they make too much out of every little difficulty they face. But when I look at the situation now, I don't have any confidence that you will feel remorse. I've also thought about the children. They have to have a mother. But I'm not sure anymore. I still can't believe you've betrayed me, but I guess there's nothing I can do but accept the fact."

"What do you want me to do?"

"If you want to go live with him, go ahead."

"Are you saying you no longer want me?"

"When a woman is so full of lust, no one can tie her down."

"I'm sorry, but I can't just go off and leave the children. Kase has called me twice on the telephone and asked me to come see him. I refused both times."

"I imagine you did this for this children's sake?"

"That was part of it."

"That's good, I suppose. I'm not trying to chase you away, you know, but you're free to think whatever you wish. My whole world has changed, and the family we were until now suddenly seems ridiculous to me. Today at the plant when I was watching the men make ham, I saw the cuts of pork hanging there and suddenly they reminded me of your body. You're just a piece of flesh. That's the way I think of you; it's come to that."

Mizue was shocked, but she had no ground for protesting. As she admitted to her husband, she had refused both times when Kase had called and urged her to come see him. Before her affair had been discovered she had been conscious of the friction generated by her reckless desires against her husband's complacency. And when she had surrendered her body to Kase, she had done so completely; but she could do so no longer. The night her husband had learned of the affair, he had taken her flesh, making her feel like a criminal, and the guilt persisted. Mizue had once been physically transformed when she accepted her lover into herself. Now all that was left after her lovemaking was a deep, heavy fatigue. She felt this would be true even if she met Kase again. Whenever she recalled that grotesque day she had slept willingly with Kase and then been taken forcefully by her husband, she felt she had to endure the consequences of her behavior. Mizue believed that, physically, she had been destroyed.

7

No matter how you look at it, it was a failure, thought Kase, regretting his visit to Eiji Shida. It was true that he had gone to Atsugi to buy trees, but he now felt it really was insolent to have visited Shida as well.

Having declined to build a garden for the conservative politician in Tokyo, Kase had no large projects lined up for autumn or winter. He had two small gardens to do, but he had left those in the hands of two students and only visited the sites occasionally to see how they were doing.

By the twentieth of October the two small gardens had been completed. Kase set out for Kyoto to look at the temple gardens there. His main objective was the garden at the Tofukuji, which still occupied his attention.

He thought all the hotels would be full since it was the height of the tourist season, but he managed to reserve a room at a pleasant hotel in Kawaramachi, near the old pleasure district downtown. If he had not been able to get a room he would have gone to Kyoto for the day and returned in the evening. It had been mid-August when he had last come to the Tofukuji, and on that occasion he had made a day trip of it.

It was evening when Kase arrived at the hotel. He lay on the bed and dozed for an hour, then showered and went out for dinner. He walked along the street, following the banks of the Takase River, looking at the signs on the shops and restaurants. He was wondering what sort of food he would like to eat, when a voice called out, "Yusaku, is that you?" It was the wife of the man who owned the Kiyoda Fish Cake Company. Standing with her was her daughter, Tamiko, and a little girl about five years old. Kase realized that this was Tamiko's daughter.

"How long have you been in Kyoto?" asked the older woman. "Well, I'm sure your work often brings you here."

"I've only just arrived," he replied, thinking it a curious coincidence that he should meet these people. The older woman wore an Oshima kimono and Tamiko wore a pantsuit. The older woman explained that they had arrived in Kyoto two days ago but were returning to Odawara in the morning.

"I was sorry to hear of your husband's death, Tamiko," said Kase.

"Thank you," she said looking down, "but all that is past now."

Since they were looking for a place to eat as well, Kase guided them to a restaurant where he often dined when he was in town. It turned out that their hotel was also quite close to his.

The next morning, while Kase was still asleep, the phone rang. It was the older woman. She explained that she was going to take her grandchild and return to Odawara right away, but that Tamiko had decided to stay one day longer in order to see the Fire Festival at Kurama that night, and she wondered if Kase would be able to spare the time to accompany her.

Kase knew that Tamiko was being pushed on him, but he agreed to go with her. He remembered that, in July, his mother had asked if he would consider marrying Tamiko. After hanging up the phone, Kase went back to sleep. It had been nine o'clock when the woman phoned him; it was nearly eleven when he woke up again. Thinking this whole encounter a curious thing, he picked up the phone and dialed the hotel where Tamiko was staying.

She answered and Kase asked whether her mother had already returned to Odawara.

"Yes, she's already gone. I'm afraid it was rather rude of her to ask you to accompany me to the festival this evening, so if you would rather not I'll understand."

"You don't need to apologize for your mother." Kase wondered how much of this had been the mother's idea; after all, Tamiko was just sitting in her hotel room waiting for him to telephone. "I can be there in about forty minutes. Will you be waiting for me in the lobby?"

Kase hung up and called the front desk to see if he could have his room for one more night, but someone else had already reserved it. He decided to just let things happen as they would. He showered, packed, and left the hotel.

He found Tamiko waiting in the hotel lobby, wearing the same outfit she had worn the night before. Seeing Kase, she stood up.

"Can I leave my bag in your room?" Kase asked. "I only had a reservation for one night and had to leave my hotel."

"I'll call the bell hop and ask him to take it up." Tamiko took Kase's bag and carried it to the front desk. As he watched her walk across the lobby, he thought again that a strange train of events was being set in motion. According to his mother, Tamiko was twenty-eight. Mizue was thirty-three. There was only five years' difference in their ages, but they were strikingly different women. Tamiko returned and they left the hotel together.

"Is there someplace you planned to go?"

"No," said Tamiko looking at the ground. "I'm sorry to be such a nuisance to you."

"It's no trouble."

"But apparently you planned to return home today."

"That was my plan, but I haven't finished my work here yet. I came to take a look at the garden at the Tofukuji. Would you like to come along?"

"Yes."

"I may go home after I have seen the garden. Are you going to stay over another night?"

"Either way is all right with me."

"What about the Fire Festival at Kurama?"

"That was my mother's idea. Actually, I had planned to go back to Odawara with her today." Tamiko's voice sounded apologetic.

"In that case, why don't I take you to the Fire Festival tonight?"

Kase felt a gentle surge of excitement as he looked at Tamiko's girlish figure.

Just as he expected, the garden at the Tofukuji was too contrived. From the abbot's quarters, they could see, on the left, a cluster of stones of various shapes and colors, including several large, horizontal ones. On the right were pine trees and a moss-covered mound. Both the stones and the gravel had a rugged, angular appearance. The garden had a certain strength about it, like a line of calligraphy written in a single stroke. When he had seen the garden before, Kase suspected that the designer had not separated himself from his design. This time, Kase thought that perhaps he had filtered out his ego after all, but had nevertheless produced this self-centered and overly simplistic garden. Still, Kase could not be certain.

"Is this the first time you've seen this garden?" Kase asked Tamiko.

"Yes, this is the first time."

"In the back they have another garden that is laid out in a checkered design. Why don't you go take a look at that?"

Kase wondered what to do next when Tamiko returned. It would be a pity to immerse her in the constricted world of a garden builder. In July, when his mother had raised the possibility of his marrying Tamiko, he had suggested that it would be more reasonable for her to marry a businessman. When Tamiko was in her early twenties he had been quite attracted to her. But he did not feel that gave him the right to seduce her now.

This was the fourth time Kase had seen this garden. On one occasion it had been a rainy winter day, but even then the garden had seemed warm and wet and throbbing with life. Even as he noticed the garden's almost sexual immediacy, he wondered what he was going to do about Tamiko.

There could be nothing false in building a garden, but the creator of a garden sometimes used falsehoods, or at least appeared to use falsehoods, in order to stimulate the imagination. The same could be said for any line of work. Among the people who created these illusions, there were some who got caught up in their own pride. Even though such a person did not expose himself consciously, people who saw his work would not be deceived. What if his subjectivity had been filtered out and he still produced this sort of garden, what then? Kase's thoughts turned to Mizue's body. She had sleek skin unmarred by discolored areas or disfigurements.

Tamiko returned.

"How did your husband die?"

"He had a liver ailment. He went into the hospital and in six days he was dead." Her reply was simple and direct. It seemed to Kase that she was artless; she did not wonder at all why he was asking such a question in a place like this.

"Shall we go somewhere for lunch?"

They had kept their taxi waiting while they looked at the garden and now used it to return to Kawaramachi. When Kase asked her what she would like for lunch, Tamiko replied that anything would be fine, so he took her to a restaurant that specialized in beef steak.

Beer was served. "You make it difficult for me when you say anything will be fine," Kase said.

Tamiko lowered her eyes. "But it's true. Anything is fine with me right now."

She did not look twenty-eight—more like mid-twenties. Kase thought of Emiko and the dark blemishes on her abdomen and wondered if Tamiko had such marks. He made up his mind that today he would let events follow their own course, whatever happened. What would they do, he wondered, when they finished eating lunch? He was already tired of sightseeing.

"Is there anything special you want to see?" he asked as they ate.

"Nothing in particular. I'll leave myself in your hands." As she said this, her face reddened.

As he cut his steak, Kase decided there was no reason for them to go to the Fire Festival. Tamiko was enjoying his company, and had seen the festival long ago. His recollection was that it was carried out in front of the Yuki Shrine at the foot of Mount Kurama north of the city. Three men carried a huge flaming pole and danced around in a large open area chanting. Since things had reached this stage, he was not enthusiastic about taking Tamiko to the festival.

After lunch they returned to Tamiko's hotel.

Tamiko's eyes were closed as Kase penetrated her body one more time, and he saw his own feelings reflected on her face. It occurred to Kase that this notion was nothing other than an assertion of his ego. What if this encounter was purely physical, with no place for introspection? Kase remained deep within her, gazing at her expression. She was clearly a different woman from Mizue. At this moment Kase could visualize the garden at the Tofukuji temple. With its naive and uncomplicated structure, the garden seemed clear and distinct. Whether or not other people realized it, this garden never changed.

8

Near the end of October, Eiji Shida began to tear down and destroy the garden Yusaku Kase had built. He dug out the stones first and scattered them throughout the garden. Every morning when Mizue awoke he was already out in the garden working. He was destroying it single-handedly.

"It isn't necessary to ruin the garden, is it?" Mizue asked one morning. Shida had just finished digging up and overturning a stone in front of their bedroom.

"What do you mean?" Shida glared at his wife and wiped the sweat from his forehead with a muddy, gloved hand.

"I don't think you are going to get any satisfaction by destroying the garden. Do you?"

"That is the most insolent thing I have ever heard. You are without shame. Do you really expect me to look at this garden every day?"

"But didn't you say I was nothing more than a slab of pork? Do you still have to destroy everything?"

"You weren't like this before. That man seduced you. Do you expect me to look out every day at the garden he built? I intend to scatter his stones, and that'll make this a completely different garden."

Mizue decided she could do nothing until Shida realized the uselessness of his efforts. She retreated into silence and watched.

Shida worked deliberately and painstakingly at tearing up the garden. As Mizue wondered what he would do about the trees, she watched him take a saw and cut off their branches. She realized that he simply wanted to obliterate the shapes Kase had created. Mizue found her husband's behavior ridiculous. She felt equally ridiculous, and thought anyone from the outside who saw them would laugh at them.

What impressed Mizue was that although Shida physically assaulted her every night and let his anger run out of control, he always maintained the role of a peaceful, dignified father in front of the children. It would not have been easy for anyone to play a respectable father's role in his situation. Mizue herself, however, began to break physically under Shida's continued attacks. She was aware of this deterioration, but felt she had no choice but to accept whatever her husband did to her. She felt he was treating her like a prostitute; she felt violated. More than a month had passed since she had last seen Kase. If only she could meet him, she believed her physical decline could be reversed and her body purified. She wanted to meet him once more, to relive that time at Hakone, so that she could again feel her inner self revealed. Her husband had sex with her almost every night, but there was no pleasure in it.

One afternoon in early November, Mizue telephoned Kase's office. It was several days before the onset of her monthly period.

At noon the next day Mizue met Kase at a hotel in the Shinagawa section of eastern Tokyo.

"You look tired," said Kase.

"It seems each day is worse than the previous one. He has completely torn the garden apart."

"That was probably inevitable. I can't criticize him for that. What I don't understand is why, when he saw us together in the hotel lobby in Shinjuku, he didn't follow us to our room and confront us there. I can't believe the amount of self-control he has."

"His company sells its products to that hotel, and he wouldn't consider jeopardizing its reputation," Mizue said.

"I see. So how are things now?"

"Everything is out of hand. He told me that if I wanted to come and live with you, I could come any time. But he doesn't really mean that."

"What are you going to do?"

"You know I'm not going to leave the children."

"But things can't go on this way; there is a limit even to Shida's patience. You will have to make a decision."

"Make a definite decision?"

"Why don't you come and live with me?"

"That's what you always say, but you know I can't because of the children. You say I have to make a decision; is that your way of saying you no longer want me?"

"No. Of course not. I need you."

"It makes me feel better to hear you say that. It's been a long time since we've seen each other. Have you taken up with any other women?"

"I've been alone the whole time."

"I don't believe you."

Mizue's mind went back over the succession of days when her husband had been assaulting her. Kase could not possibly have gone without sex so long.

"Since I had no woman, I had no choice but to be by myself."

Mizue said nothing more, but she could not rid herself of the suspicion that Kase was lying.

They recreated their Hakone experience, and during her time with Kase, Mizue found some reprieve from her sense of physical decline. Once back to reality, she asked, "Don't you think I've changed?"

"You seem a little haggard, but otherwise you're the same."

"I'm glad to hear you say so."

"Is Shida giving you a pretty hard time? Physically, I mean."

"Yes, he is, but I'd rather not talk about it."

"I suppose it's inevitable."

Kase told her about how he had separated from Emiko when she was twenty-five and then had taken up with her again when she was in her thirties. He recalled his jealousy at the mastery of sex she had achieved through a man he did not know.

"But you should have expected that," said Mizue.

"I don't think you have any idea what that feeling is like, since Shida was never unfaithful to you."

When they parted that afternoon, Mizue took the train from Shinagawa to return home. On the way she wondered if she would be jealous if her husband took up with another woman.

No matter how she thought about it, she was not certain what her reaction would be.

9

It was shortly before noon on Sunday morning. Kase was at home in Hodogaya and had just finished the box lunch sent in by the restaurant. He had the morning paper spread out before him and was smoking a cigarette when Tamiko showed up. While they were together in Kyoto he had given her his address and said he was home on Sundays.

Tamiko took off her coat and sat down in a chair.

"So," Kase said, "you decided to come after all." In Kyoto he had told her that he could not make any promises about their future.

"It seemed like I had to come," said Tamiko, her face reddening.

"Don't you have any plans to remarry?"

"Well, there's some talk."

"You're not so enthusiastic, is that it?"

"I'm not much interested in businessmen anymore."

"It's not your fault you can't put your heart into it. I don't suppose you've eaten lunch yet."

"I'm not hungry."

"Afterward I'll take you out to Chinatown, how about that? When you got home from Kyoto, did you tell your mother about us?"

"No. Mother didn't say anything, and I didn't either."

"What about your husband, was that a love match?"

"No. It was an arranged marriage."

"How long were you married?"

"Six years," Tamiko said. "Why are you asking all these questions?"

"Well, you just don't seem very grown up to me, but of course it's not your fault."

"Well, if that's the way you feel, I mean, if you think I'm not good enough."

"That's not what I mean."

This woman is also like a garden path, thought Kase, recalling Tamiko's firm body as he had experienced it in Kyoto. The path is laid out in a straight line now, but it won't be long until the stones are scattered; left, right, left, right.

There are all sorts of garden paths. Kase prided himself on having built a number of them, but the thought of following one of those paths all the way to the end made him uneasy. Though the path was narrow, it seemed infinitely long. He wondered if his uneasiness would be finally dispelled once he reached the tea house at the end of the path and entered it. No, it would not. It was easy enough to follow the garden path, but the tiny three-mat room at the end gave the impression instead of being infinitely large. It made him uneasy inside there. Some said the designer's job was to build the garden path, and that at the entrance to the tea room his responsibility stopped. Kase, however, did not think this way. To him the garden path was an extension of the tea room, and the two were connected.

Even after Tamiko appeared, it was Mizue who lived within Kase. No matter what Shida did to destroy the garden, nothing could change the fact it had been Mizue's inspiration that built it. And even if he did destroy it, the garden in all its aspects, summer and autumn, winter and spring, would remain in Mizue's heart and memory.

Tamiko was just as tense as she had been in Kyoto, but Kase sensed she was gradually beginning to loosen up. After a time, when he entered her again, there was no question that she had relaxed. He could see himself reflected in Tamiko's features, just as he had in Kyoto. Perhaps what he saw reflected there was a violent, explosive force. Lying there inside Tamiko he could visualize the artless garden of the Tofukuji, and could truly believe in his own power.

Tamiko's husband had been a year older. They had been married from the time she was twenty-two until she was twenty-seven, and when she thought back over their life together, it seemed as though they had only been playing house. He had run his own business under the patronage of his parents, and there had been no difficulties or hardships for them at all.

On the train returning to Odawara, Tamiko's thoughts went back to the time before her marriage. When she was barely twenty she had looked on the thirty-year-old Yusaku as a grown man. She had heard from her mother that Yusaku Kase studied all the time and paid no attention to his wife, and for that reason two of his wives had deserted him. She remembered visiting Kase's home, seeing him drinking beer and looking exhausted. If she called out a greeting to him, he merely grunted a vague and meaningless reply. Her mother said the family business would go to his younger brother because Kase himself had no interest in it.

No sooner had she returned home to Odawara last spring, after her husband's death, than her mother began saying how wonderful it would be if Yusaku Kase would marry her. Only then did she remember him. She had not even thought of him since her marriage.

She had been surprised at meeting Kase in Kyoto. To a twenty-eight-year-old woman, a forty-year-old man still seemed old. Tamiko's mother had instructed her to stay over in Kyoto an extra day, and she was willing enough; their families had ties.

She recalled that in Kyoto Kase had said he couldn't make any promise about the future.

She had said she knew that. She wondered now if he had been living by himself ever since his second wife had left him.

This was only the second time they had made love, but the sensation of a man's weight was familiar to Tamiko. But with Kase it was an experience unlike any she had ever had with her husband, even though they had produced a child. Tamiko wondered what made sex with Kase so special. This was only the second time she had given herself to him, but something had come to life within her.

Tamiko had helped in the store and kitchen since she'd come home in the spring. There were employees to do those jobs, so there wasn't much to fill the long hours. Next year her daughter, Taeko, would be in school.

As the train approached Odawara, Tamiko began to wonder if she would make a habit of going to see Kase on Sundays. Quite apart from the pleasant sensation of having a man's weight on her, she felt there would be no escaping this attachment. A new world was opening up.

After several days Tamiko knew for sure she was being driven by a powerful impulse. She had not been aware of it when she visited Kase on Sunday; it had merely seemed an extension of their chance encounter in Kyoto. But she now felt it very keenly. She longed to feel the weight of a man's body.

THE FLOW

(Moronobu's "Predatory" Garden)

1

During the Genroku period (1688–1703) the Ukiyoe artist Moronobu Hishikawa wrote *Yokeizukuri Niwa no Zu* or "Instructions for the Creation of a Full-View Garden." The book was published when Moronobu was about fifty and his erotic prints were being widely sold. Kase had no idea why a printmaker would write a book about gardens, but there were ideas here that only such an artist could have conceived, and Kase found that interesting. Since Moronobu was a printmaker, naturally the book was illustrated, and the drawings were well executed.

In his book Moronobu says:

> It is good to have something predatory in a garden with lawns. Stones should be arranged in a broad, open garden, but there should be neither potted plants nor flowering shrubs. If one puts out seed in the evening to attract birds so that they can be caught, the following day there will be geese, quail, and other small birds, and dinner guests will find hawks. Randomly placed stones are to be placed here and there. The garden will be based on scenery like that found at Matsushima, with its many tiny pine-clad islands. It has no stepping stones, but rather the appearance of a field.

Such a garden interested Kase. When Moronobu spoke of a lawn garden, he did not mean the usual kind of lawn, but wild grass, according to his illustration. The stones were arranged in groups, and from the drawing one got the impression of the sea and seashore. In this sort of garden the grass could be seen as grass, or it could be imagined to be the sea. Seen simply as grass, the garden recalled Basho's poem:

> Taken ill on a journey
> And still my dreams roam about
> Over withered fields.

Moronobu said the garden should resemble the coast at Matsushima.

In that regard it was not much different from a dry landscape garden. But Kase preferred to see it as a withered field. He was also intrigued by the idea of using arrangements of stones to attract birds. Even today, with no shrubs, but only grass and stones, the birds would perch on the stones.

Kase did not know if there had actually been such a garden in the Genroku period, but when he considered Moronobu as a garden designer, he sensed this garden must have expressed the inner desolation of the artist. Kase also liked the idea of a garden that would be enjoyed by predators. The predators would kill more than just geese and quail. Kase could visualize Mizue or Tamiko seated on the stones in such a garden. Sitting on the stones they would look quite different from how they would if they were following the path to a tea house.

With Tamiko Kase had envisioned the overly simple garden of the temple Tofukuji, a garden that still produced a sense of repose. In contrast, Moronobu's garden flowed. When Kase saw the Tofukuji garden, Moronobu's garden had naturally come to mind. Moronobu's garden was fluid, and had motion, but in the end Kase was not sure whether Moronobu's garden might not be the process by which the garden of the Tofukuji was achieved. What was clear to him was that the two gardens resembled each other in many respects. Moronobu's book had designs for other gardens as well, and all of them had this same fluidity, this natural sense of flow. Among the garden designs in his book, only the predatory lawn garden made one conscious of the bleak desolation of the artist's mind. The connection between the Moronobu who made erotic prints and the Moronobu who designed this garden was clear.

Tamiko visited Kase three more times before the middle of December. On the third visit Kase reminded her once again that he could not make any promises about their future.

"That's all right," she replied. "I won't make any problems for you." She answered in the same forlorn voice he had heard in Kyoto.

After she left it struck Kase, as it had on the previous Sunday, how Tamiko was retiring and pensive by nature. Having known her since she was a child, it was hard for him to think of her now as grown up. Compared to the richness of Mizue's flesh, there was something pathetic about Tamiko's body.

In Moronobu's predatory lawn garden there were two clusters of stones. Kase envisioned Mizue seated on the near cluster and Tamiko seated on the far one. He imagined in the garden a man going back and forth between the two women. The unsettled state of the garden reflected the bleak desolation of the man.

2

The garden at the Shida home had become rather odd looking. Returning from the plant at Atsugi one evening, Eiji Shida looked at the garden he had destroyed and felt it symbolized the ruined relationship with his wife. There did not seem to be any way they could return to their former way of life. He had realized from the outset that to destroy the garden would accomplish nothing. All that remained was a sense of futility. In mid-November his wife told him she had spent the previous day with Kase. Hearing her declaration, he could not even bring himself to be angry. For the first time he felt like simply giving up.

"Are you planning to go live with him?"

"I can't do that. I have the children to think of."

"Then I guess that's it. I don't know what to do, either. When I think what it would be like for my children to be without a mother, I wonder if it would be better just to go on like this, pretending nothing's happening. I've considered all sorts of actions, but I can't think of any way to resolve this. Maybe if you just left I'd be able to see what has to be done. I've been thinking about the children, just as you have. I had thought that at least for their sake we could come to some understanding, but even that doesn't seem possible now. Let's just let the matter drop for a while. You have to understand, of course, that things may change for me even if you choose not to leave this family."

Eiji stared at his wife, who stood in front of him saying, without remorse, that she had been seeing another man. He wondered what would happen to him if he lost sight of his own moral sense and family responsibility.

Shida gazed for a time at the ruined garden. Neither the children nor

Momoko seemed to realize something was wrong between husband and wife. And when the time came and they had to know, it would be his duty to tell them. But he would protect them from it as long as he could. With this resolve he turned and went into the house.

Mizue counted the days since she had met Kase at the hotel in Shinagawa and found that a month had passed. She was uncertain what to do now. She could not break with Kase no matter how selfish her behavior appeared to her husband. At Shinagawa they had recreated their lovemaking at Hakone. Mizue tried to deny that it was merely for sex, but when she was apart from Kase she was conscious of her own physical deterioration. Her husband no longer assaulted her. Since destroying the garden he had sometimes kept to his own bed for a week at a time. She was puzzled until it occurred to her that he too was aware of her decline. She wondered if he had taken up with some other woman, but that did not seem likely.

Birds still came to the withered garden to look for food. Despite the destruction, Kase's basic design remained. It was a curious garden, but to someone who did not know what had happened, it would not look ruined. The stones that Shida had dug up and strewn about were washed by the rain and took on a tranquil look that was almost natural. Even the trees with their branches broken did not look contrived. Mizue wondered if she too would have to go on living in much the same condition as the garden.

Standing in the garden, Mizue looked through the window at the clock inside the house. It was nearly noon. She walked to the hall telephone and dialed Kase's office. The person who answered informed her that Kase had a cold and was not at the office that day.

This was the first time she had visited him at Hodogaya. Mizue looked up at the six-story apartment building situated in a valley between the hills. She thought it strange that so robust a person as Kase should miss work on account of a cold.

Climbing to the sixth floor she found Kase's door and pressed the buzzer. A woman who appeared somewhat younger than Mizue answered the door. Emiko would be older than this.

"I'm Mrs. Shida," said Mizue. The woman disappeared for a moment, then returned and invited Mizue in.

Mizue handed the woman the bunch of chrysanthemums she had brought, still wondering who this could be. She had no idea.

She was shown to a room and a short time later Kase appeared from the adjoining room wearing a dressing gown.

"I've been down with the flu," he said.

"Who's she?" asked Mizue in a whisper. The other woman had gone to the kitchen.

"Oh, she's a relative of mine. Her family makes fish cakes at Odawara just like mine does," he replied.

Presently the woman brought tea and said, "I'll be going now, Yusaku."

"Are you. Well, thanks. I'll be up and around tomorrow, so you needn't come."

"All right."

When she was gone Mizue said, "She's quite attractive, isn't she."

"Do you think so? I've known her since she was a little girl; it never occurred to me that she was pretty. It's been a month since you and I've seen each other. How have things been for you?"

"He's torn the garden completely apart. Things seem to be taking a turn for the worse in several ways."

"Is he still forcing himself on you?"

"Not since he tore up the garden."

"When you say things are taking a turn for the worse, do you mean Shida has lost his feeling for you?"

"I don't know. It just seems there is nothing we can do. Both of us still feel deeply attached to the children."

"So all you can do is look out at the ruins."

"That's right. Before I called your office this morning, I looked at the garden, and it seemed to me that I'm in much the same condition."

Kase smoked his cigarette and said nothing. He coughed briefly, then stood up and said, "Shall we go in the other room?"

Later as Mizue made love to him she had a vision of the desolate, ruined garden. The more she thought about it, the more it seemed the garden shared her condition: it could neither die nor go on living.

114

3

The senior members of the staff at the Atsugi plant were holding a year-end celebration at the Tsurumaki hot springs resort just a few miles east of Hadano. Even though it was a small resort, there were more than a hundred geisha working there. Shida planned to attend.

"I hear those geisha will do it with anyone," declared the plant director, Fujioka, as they set out.

The party began at six o'clock with eighteen people. Eight geisha, all of them young, spent their entire time serving saké and talking with the guests; another group of three older geisha went from party to party to play music and dance.

Shida had never been much involved in the entertainment world, but now he was enjoying the sight of the young geisha. How nice to be youthful, he thought; he had never felt this way before. Shida inquired, and learned that all the geisha were in their early twenties.

Halfway through the dinner party Shida noticed the girl sitting next to him. They probably aren't all promiscuous, he thought. Her name was Eiko, and when he considered her cool demeanor, he decided she must already have a steady patron. She had a large build and a rather small face, and looked about twenty-five.

"You seem to be the most cool and composed girl here," Shida said.

"I'm not surprised you think so," replied Eiko. "I'm the oldest here."

"Have you been in the business that long?"

"I retired once, but came back to work this fall."

Shida returned to Tsurumaki the following evening, took a room for himself at a small inn, and called Eiko. Eiko seemed surprised to see him when she arrived.

"You're probably not happy to see last night's guest again today."

"What makes you say that? It's all business to me."

"You said you'd left the profession and then come back."

"Yes, I lost my husband, so I've come back for good."

The woman was frank and open. As they drank saké, Eiko told him of her past. In the spring three years before, she had become the wife of an accountant, but when he died last January she had been turned out of the house by his first wife's children. She returned to her parents' home and then, in the autumn, had resumed her career as a geisha.

"Say, are you the one who married Sawada?"

"Oh, how did you know?" Eiko sat up a little more formally.

"He used to do business with my company. I heard he had taken a second wife, but no one seemed to know who she was."

"That's because I had been a geisha; he never introduced me to anyone."

No wonder she had seemed so unruffled the night before. Shida looked at her with new eyes.

"Do you come here often?" she asked.

"No. As a matter of fact I never come here. It's just that I remembered you from last night. Does that seem strange to you?"

"Not at all. I'm not here on Mondays, but I'd be pleased if you'd call for me again."

"Is Monday your day off?"

"I go home to visit my parents in the country. Do you know Udoko?"

"Yes, very well. Our maid, Momoko, comes from there."

"Is that Momoko from the locksmith's family?"

"Yes."

"Oh, this is embarrassing. You must be the Shida from the ham company. Please excuse me, I had no idea where my husband worked or what he did. All I knew was that he had five men working for him. I was more like a maid than a wife; I spent all my time in the kitchen. My family is related to Momoko's. In a small village like that, of course, everyone is related to everyone else."

It seemed that Eiko was becoming more relaxed.

"Isn't that something. So you're a native of Udoko. Me and that paper-making village go back a long way together. Did your family make paper in the old days?"

"They still make paper; in fact, our family's the only one in the village that still does. All the young people are leaving there. I have two older brothers; one lives in Tokyo with his family, and the other in Yokohama. Only my parents keep up the tradition, so when they die there will be no one left to do it."

"I heard they're going to build a dam on the upper reaches of the Nakatsu River."

"If they do, it'll be the end of paper making. When I go home on Mondays, I spend my time until noon on Tuesday helping with the paper. You probably find it odd that a geisha would spend her time on handmade paper."

"No, that's not odd at all. It's a good story. I may start coming here and calling on you to entertain me. I've lived in this area all my life, but I don't know much about how geisha operate in a hot springs resort. Do you work for a geisha house?"

"No. Even at the time I stopped working three years ago I was free-lance. I have an apartment of my own. During the day I give samisen lessons there, but the young geisha these days don't work very hard at their art."

"You look about twenty-five."

"Why, what a thing to say. I'm almost thirty."

"Oh really? I didn't hear you play the samisen last night."

"Last night I interrupted another engagement to come to your party. One of the younger geisha pointed you out as a very prominent person and suggested I go sit next to you, so I did. No one asked me to play samisen last night. Besides, they were singing military and popular songs. Young geisha prefer them because they don't need a samisen accompaniment."

Eiko said she had heard the Shida Ham Company was sponsoring a year-end party, but thought it would be only for the regular employees. And since Shida himself did not normally come to this resort for entertainment, she naturally had not recognized him at the party.

Shida spent two hours there that evening drinking saké and left the inn feeling quite good. He felt he had been comforted.

4

Ever since her visit to Hodogaya, Mizue suspected there was an inscrutable quality to Kase; she did not really know him. As they made love at his apartment, the withered, ruined garden came before her eyes. The garden was neither alive nor dead, yet it retained the primary features Kase had created. Although Shida had tried to destroy the garden, it had survived. The stones had been dug up and scattered, but they remained Kase's eyes. No matter how or where they were placed, the stones watched her. Shida would occasionally move them about. The large stones were too heavy to move by hand, so he would place a pole under them and lever them along the ground. Mizue watched but pretended not to. There was no way he could transform this garden with his bare hands, no matter how hard he tried. The garden was still Kase's.

Mizue's mind went back to something Kase had said to Shida when he built the garden: "It isn't wise to fool around with the randomly placed stones; they are what give a garden vitality." The stones that had been displaced had now come to exist as stones randomly strewn about the garden.

Mizue could not understand why she found no hope in her relationship with Kase even when they were together. When he asked her to leave her children and come to him, he gave no indication that such an arrangement would work. Certainly Mizue herself had no hope. Uneasiness haunted her constantly. Lately she had thought more than ever about her father, her mother, and her brother who had died, and at times she had ominous feelings about herself. When she had not seen Kase for a time and her thirst for him was unbearable, she wondered if this was not after all a desire to die, and her suffering increased. The events of her life had caused her to wish for death. This feeling had grown within Mizue ever since she had come to know Kase. Her anxiety was becoming ever more clearly defined.

Every year as winter approached, Momoko's family in Udoko sent cabbages, radishes, burdock, onions, and carrots for the Shidas to use at New Year's. They also sent along a small, tightly packed cask of radish pickles.

This year, as usual, Momoko's elder brother arrived in a small truck loaded with vegetables. He dug a hole in the yard behind the kitchen and buried the onions and some of the other vegetables to keep them fresh. Every year Mizue gave him ham and sausages to take home in return.

After he had gone, Mizue stood staring at the pile of fresh vegetables.

She turned and looked back at her broken home, thinking only that it would be a gloomy New Year's season. Recently her husband was late getting home from work. Twice, he had not come home at all. Both times he had apparently gone directly to the office the next morning.

Shida never explained why he did not come home, and Mizue never asked. There was nothing she could do if her husband took another woman. Not only did Shida not explain why he stayed away, he didn't act as though anything was wrong. When he returned home late, he came by taxi. Mizue supposed he had been drinking. She remained aloof from her husband.

Shida stayed away all night a third time. Mizue got up the next morning and gazed out at the garden, convinced now that her husband had another woman. Did they now feel apathy toward each other? Her uneasiness increased. As husband and wife, they had two children. The children could not remain mere spectators to what was happening with their parents.

Three wrens were flitting from branch to branch among the bare trees. Just as she noticed them darting from branch to branch, they suddenly flew away down the river. These birds would depart from the mountains when spring came. Mizue realized that with the gloomy arrival of the new year she would be thirty-four years old. On the night she and her husband first talked about her affair with Kase, she had said her lover didn't have to have been Kase. She was unsure now whether she believed that. Many things now seemed unclear. Kase had never offered any hope their relationship would work out, and even now she could not let herself depend on him. Perhaps it was true that she would have been better off with someone else.

For some time now she had not really talked with her husband. It had been more than ten days since Shida had come to her bed. Perhaps he had found some way to soothe his wounds. After all, he had suggested they let the matter drop for a while, and had said that even if she didn't go to Kase, there was always the chance that things might change for him.

Once again the group of wrens appeared and flitted busily among the trees.

5

As soon as Kase got up, he took a shower and set about making tea, only to find that there was none left. He dressed and went out to buy some. No sooner had he returned from buying tea and cigarettes than Tamiko showed up.

"Did you go out to eat?"

"No, I'd run out of tea."

"Well, you have tea in the kitchen," said Tamiko, bringing out the package of tea.

"Oh, I didn't know it was there."

"I'll make it."

Kase liked to steep a good-quality loose green tea in boiling water. He never used the tea more than twice before discarding it, so a pound would only last about ten days. Apparently Tamiko had learned his method of making tea since she had been coming to see him.

"I have no right to ask, but who was that woman who showed up last time I was here?" asked Tamiko. She set the cup of tea in front of Kase.

"I think it was Mrs. Shida. I don't really know." Kase took a sip of the tea. "This is delicious."

"What do you mean, you don't really know?"

"Tami, when you ask me who she is, you don't just mean her name and address."

"But what sort of woman would come to visit a bachelor's apartment?" asked Tamiko, lowering her eyes.

"You're just thinking of yourself and saying that."

"But I can't help it." Tamiko twisted her hands in her lap and continued to stare at the floor. Sometimes she wore a kimono and sometimes Western clothes; today she was wearing white slacks with a black suede jacket.

"She comes from a decent family, she's a housewife with two children. She's thirty-three years old. Do you want me to say anything more?"

"No, never mind, that's enough." Quietly Tamiko got up and went to the kitchen.

Kase lit a cigarette. Tamiko brought in plate of sandwiches.

"I left home early this morning, so I stopped downtown to get these." Kase recognized the sandwich wedges from a shop in Motomachi.

"Thanks. Is your mother saying anything about us these days?" asked Kase, taking a sandwich from the plate.

"My mother? No, nothing," said Tamiko, fetching more tea.

This young woman was coming here regularly, as though operated by remote control. It's kind of odd, thought Kase. Whenever the girl shows up, I have visions of the garden at Tofukuji.

Ever since envisioning the two women seated on stones in Moronobu's predatory garden, Kase realized he had devoted too much of himself to building gardens and had come out the loser in real life. Haven't I been oblivious to my failure because I believed too much in my own explosive power? he thought. Maybe saying that building gardens is a struggle against the commonplace is really saying that I have become detached from life.

Kase's struggle was also a struggle against himself. During the course of this striving, Emiko had left him, and Kazue had also deserted him. That both his wives had gone was a clear indication he was out of touch with what was real. Not only that, Emiko had fallen so low that even after she remarried, she still came to see Kase from time to time, and he felt responsible. But in his struggle against the mundane he had at last met a real woman. On meeting Mizue he had to ask himself whether his feelings for her were honest. Didn't he find her attractive simply because she understood his work and could accept it? Kase thought of the time Mizue had come to see him just before he left for Yamagata. He had told her then how he felt about meeting such a woman. The following day Emiko had called him at his office, and when he went to the hotel to meet her, he had a vision of his own corrupted flesh. He had hoped Mizue would be able to purify him. But when he looked at Tamiko, he thought perhaps Mizue was no different from the other women who, like streams, had flowed across his life. Would Tamiko be the one to cleanse him?"

"Tami, I wonder how closely we are related by blood," said Kase, biting into his third sandwich.

"I think your grandfather and my grandmother were brother and sister. That would make us second cousins."

"Second cousins, is it? Are you spending New Year's with your family?"

"Yes. How about you?"

"I usually spend the holidays at a hotel. All the stores are closed, so it's the only thing to do. In the old days, though, I used to go home to Odawara."

"What are your plans this year?"

"Let's see, it's already the twentieth. I'd better make a hotel reservation soon." Kase wondered which hotel he might choose this year.

Closing her eyes, Tamiko thought, This is not just any man's weight I feel, this is Yusaku's weight. I am reassured when he is with me. When I go home to Odawara, I have my parents there and my brothers and my child, and yet I have the feeling that I am alone, with no one to look out for me. Coming here is like waking from sleep. When we were in Kyoto it was like slowly waking from a deep sleep, but the first time I came here, the sleep seemed to be pushed back as far as it would go, as though I was fully awake. It's like that every time I come here. If I am now so awake it only shows how deeply asleep I was.

In accepting this man's weight today, Tamiko had become truly aware of herself. Her own freedom had been closed away in a dark and secret place, but the more she felt his weight upon her, the more she wanted to seek out this dark place where freedom had been hidden.

"You could spend the New Year's holiday here if you wanted," said Tamiko modestly, after they had made love.

"It's too much trouble to have to cook for myself."

"I don't suppose you would want to have me here with you."

"What about your child?

"My mother and father will go off to the Izu Peninsula for the holiday. I can send her with them."

"I guess in that case it will be all right if you come here. Shall we plan on it?"

"Yes, let's."

"When will your parents leave for Izu?"

"On the thirtieth, so I'll come here then."

Kase felt her warm breath as she snuggled close to him. There was a freshness about her earnest, taut figure. He had no plan for how to deal with his situation, for it seemed now that both Tamiko and Mizue were indispensable to him.

6

When Shida first called Eiko to him at the small hot springs resort inn, he had felt comforted by her presence, but he never thought things would turn out like this.

The third time he had gone to the same place to meet her, he had spoken to the proprietress of the inn before Eiko arrived and asked if Eiko was a geisha with a reputation.

"No. Not at all. That girl is very proper. Why she's so proper she even got herself established as someone's second wife," said the proprietress, apparently horrified that anyone would consider Eiko promiscuous.

That evening Shida told Eiko he would like to become her regular customer. He would plan to come several times a month if that was all right with her.

"That's very good for me, but it might be awkward for you since you live so near," said Eiko, obviously aware of his situation.

Following this conversation Shida bought a condominium in Hiratsuka. The price was reasonable. The apartment was available because the building faced west, with bad light in the morning hours. Shida asked Eiko to put up with the darkness. Shida had found a rather exclusive place because he feared his coming and going might attract attention if Eiko was in an ordinary apartment.

Three days a week Eiko left the apartment at noon and took the bus to Tsurumaki. She had arranged to give regular samisen lessons to the apprentice geisha at the geisha exchange office there, which was next door to the apartment she had been renting before she moved to Hiratsuka.

The location of Eiko's new apartment was also convenient for Shida since he could take Highway 129 directly to Atsugi. On days when he went to the plant at Hiratsuka, it was so close he could sleep in. One evening Shida recalled that Eiko was only twenty-eight and asked her indirectly whether she had accepted any lovers in the two years since her husband had died.

"No," she replied. "How could I have?"

Before he married Mizue, Shida had played around a little, but he had never been very enthusiastic about it. A serious and solemn man of thirty-eight, he had never before encountered a woman like Eiko, who had been raised in the geisha world. Since his marriage to Mizue, Shida had never paid attention to other women, but with Eiko, his male desire was aroused for the first time. In the beginning he had gone to see Eiko simply in retaliation for his wife's infidelity, but now clearly there was more to it than that. There was comfort and satisfaction. Once he realized he was not just subject to a passing mood, he decided to see how far these feelings of his could go.

Eiko's attitude toward life was fastidious, and from a man's point of view she seemed very reliable. Eiko said that all the young geisha were selfish, but Eiko herself was quite old-fashioned. Shida had never had a chance to be around this sort of traditional working girl before. On the day Shida had gone to Hodogaya, he told Kase that everyone makes mistakes sometimes, and that if we make too much of those mistakes, it is impossible to live. Consequently, he had planned to help his wife correct her wayward behavior. At the time he had actually believed this possible, but in fact it hadn't been. He had assumed at first that Mizue had been seduced and deceived by her lover. A deception he could have opened her eyes to. Instead, Mizue began to reveal a kind of feminine insolence that Shida was unable to comprehend. On the morning he had set about destroying the garden, his wife had told him that even if he succeeded he would not feel satisfied. At this point he had begun to see his wife as a stranger. Could the woman who had borne him two children possibly have changed so radically? Shida had to view the world from a new perspective.

After he had begun living with Eiko at Hiratsuka, Shida felt he was able to put some distance between himself and his wife's body. He no longer felt any desire for her; all that remained was bitterness.

It was Sunday morning. Eiko was already up and fixing breakfast while Shida lay smoking a cigarette before getting out of bed. Since the apartment building faced west, he could not see the sea from the window. Instead, directly before him towered Mount Koma at Oiso. Although the two towns adjoined each other, Oiso was sheltered by the mountain to the north and remained warm in winter, while Hiratsuka was on flat land stretching all the way to the foot of the Tanzawa range and was quite cold.

Although she and Shida had a panel heater, Eiko, according to her custom, lit charcoal in the hibachi and set an iron tea kettle over the fire. Eiko did not like the Western dining room, so she placed their table in a small, Japanese-style room. She said she could never feel comfortable unless she was sitting on tatami mats.

"Today is Sunday; is it all right for you to be away from home today?" called Eiko from the kitchen after she had washed her face.

"You don't have to worry about that."

Shida appreciated her sensitivity, but did not feel like talking about his family in Hadano. Ever since he had set Eiko up in this apartment, he had wanted to avoid the ill feeling and confusion at home. He had tried to destroy the garden Kase built, but it had not done any good, and since he had taken up with Eiko, he had come to see how foolish he had been.

Mizue was the sort of woman who would cross the main stream of a river, even though the flow was blocked, creating small or narrower channels. Eiko, on the other hand, would entrust herself to the smaller channels. Shida was keenly aware of this difference in their natures.

After he had washed his face and returned to the bedroom, Shida could smell the aroma of miso soup.

It was a cold morning for Mizue. When her husband had been angry and tearing up the garden, she knew he was conscious of her. Now that he was completely ignoring her, she felt just like the ruined garden. The garden could be viewed as a kind of abstract painting, and Mizue saw herself as a woman depicted in such a painting.

"Has daddy gone on a business trip?" Noriko had asked Mizue at the breakfast table.

"It's near the end of the year, so he is very busy."

"When the end of the year approaches, they have to make ham even on Sundays," her son, Eiichi, had said, looking at his sister.

125

As her husband was staying away more frequently now, Mizue felt that things would probably become even more chaotic at home. Her mind went back to the year she was twenty-nine, the year she had seen three caskets carried away. It had only been five years ago, but it seemed much longer. It was nearly the twenty-sixth of December, the anniversary of her brother's death. She never failed to go to the temple on that day. Last year and the year before, on the important third anniversary of his death, even her brother's family had not bothered to come. Mizue had sent a letter to them in Tokyo proposing that they go together to sponsor special services at the time of the autumn equinox, but the letter had been returned stamped "Addressee Unknown." All that remained after her brother had committed suicide were debts, and Mizue could imagine what life was like for his widow with two children to care for. As each year drew to a close, she thought about her sister-in-law and felt depressed.

The day was overcast, making her feel colder and more forlorn. Shortly after noon Mizue sent Momoko out on an errand and then telephoned Hodogaya.

"I want to meet you tomorrow." Mizue felt especially desperate, since her husband no longer cared.

"I could manage it on the twenty-sixth," Kase replied. Mizue said she had to go to the cemetery at Oiso on the twenty-sixth. It could not be helped.

"Come to my office in Shibuya later that day," Kase told her, "whenever it's convenient."

She could call from someplace near his office and he would meet her.

It was past three o'clock when Shida returned home. He quickly changed clothes and went out to wash the car. Neither husband nor wife said a word to the other; they were each wrapped in their own thoughts. The husband had been out all night and spoke not a word of explanation, and the wife did not even bother to question him. The family was completely destroyed, and Mizue knew she was the one who had destroyed it. Even if she met Kase on the twenty-sixth, nothing would be resolved. She decided to leave early that day to go to Oiso, and afterward Tokyo.

W I N D

(The Abbot's Garden at Tofukuji)

1

On the afternoon of December thirtieth Tamiko arrived at Hodogaya with a bundle of materials for preparing the special holiday dishes. Kase looked into the kitchen and saw her busily preparing the food. "Tami, do you really know what you're doing?" he asked.

"What sort of fool do you think I am? I've known how to do this since I was a girl. I could even fix black soybeans when I was seventeen."

"Well, that's lucky for me. It looks like I'm going to have some good things to eat this New Year's." Previously when Tamiko had come to him here, he had been reminded of the garden at the Tofukuji. But it seemed odd that this feeling had nothing to do with his having first made love to her on the day they had gone to see that garden. If Mizue is immoral, then I must be too, he thought. Tamiko's purity shows both Mizue and me for what we really are. Perhaps this has something to do with my seeing her as the living embodiment of the Tofukuji garden.

"What reason did you give your family for not staying home for the holiday?" asked Kase.

"I told my brother and his wife I was going on a trip with friends. My mother won't say anything to them."

Tamiko, who came to him quietly and intimately, had a sense of a continuous flow of time within her. "How does your family usually celebrate the New Year?"

"One time we went for a trip, but usually we stay home. It's our custom to worship at the Taishi Temple at Kawasaki. How about you, do you go anywhere to worship?" Tamiko asked.

"I usually spend the New Year's holiday sleeping. I'm afraid I long ago cut all my ties with both the Buddhas and the Shinto gods."

Ever since his youth Kase had spent the holidays in bed. After separating from his second wife he had found it too much bother to conform to society, and even before that he had not been in the habit of going out on holidays.

Tamiko put the black beans in water. While they cooked, she sewed two rusty nails into a bag and, following the old custom, added the bag to the bean pot. This was supposed to make the beans tender, and Tamiko faithfully preserved the tradition.

"I don't suppose it would work if you didn't add rusty nails?" asked Kase, watching her.

"That's right. I've tried it without the nails and the beans always turn out hard and wrinkled. People had strange ways in the old days, but they work."

"I was thinking we might go to Chinatown for dinner tonight, but I guess we can't go out while the beans are cooking."

"Oh no, let's go out. I'll just drain the beans, and I can cook them later tonight." Tamiko glanced up and Kase was startled by the intensity of her look. How gentle are a woman's eyes before she realizes how determined she is, he thought.

On the twenty-sixth, Kase had met Mizue at Shibuya. "I fear I'm reaching the point where I want to destroy myself," Mizue had said.

Kase had asked Mizue if she couldn't try to be more optimistic. Yet her comment conveyed to him the extent of her emotional desolation. Even if he advised her to be hopeful, Mizue said, she could not.

When he was with Tamiko, Kase was more conscious than ever of Mizue's sensitivity, and again today there came to his mind the two clusters of stones in Moronobu's predatory garden. Even though Tamiko was there before his eyes, all he could see was the barren landscape of his own inner desolation.

2

Shida had decided to spend New Year's eve and New Year's day at Hadano with his family. Since Eiko had to go back to work on the fifth, he stayed with her from the second until the morning she left. This was the first time he had been away from home for so many days in succession. The Shida Ham Company also observed the holiday until the fourth of January, so he thought it would be all right if he went directly to the plant on the morning of the fifth. Just before the holidays began he had told the plant foremen at both Atsugi and Hiratsuka that he would not be home on the third and that they should not feel obliged to pay a New Year's greeting call at his home.

It was the afternoon of January fourth. Shida had taken a late morning bath and gone out on the veranda. After spending days with Eiko, his body felt sodden with her essence. From the veranda he could see the ocean. Mount Koma rose just before his eyes and as he turned and looked north, he could see the Tanzawa massif towering in the winter sunlight. The town of Oiso spread out beneath his feet. Oiso was unpleasant to Shida now. Mizue had been born and raised there. Hadano was also disagreeable. Except for his two children, he wanted no part of the town.

"You will take a chill being out there after your bath," called Eiko, and he came inside. "Shall I prepare saké for you?" she asked, setting the table in the small Japanese-style room.

"Yes, thank you." Shida found his cigarettes and went to join Eiko.

An iron kettle boiled on the hibachi. Eiko handed Shida a bottle of saké, and he placed it in the kettle.

"It's not so nice here, having a view to the west. Why don't you quit being a geisha. We'll set you up in a place of your own." Shida said this as he watched Eiko's busy hands grinding horseradish to eat with their fish cakes.

"That would be nice, but will it be all right for you to do something like that?" replied Eiko, serving the horseradish onto plates.

"You can't go on working at the hot springs resort forever."

"You may be right about that."

After her husband, Sawada, had died, and Sawada's children had forced her to leave the house, Eiko had never received help from anyone. It was not just that she wanted to avoid a quarrel; rather, she simply wanted nothing for herself. Shida knew that Eiko would be quite happy if he bought a place for her, and that it was not worth it to her if it caused trouble with his wife.

"I could set you up in a little restaurant. Not one of those red-light joints, but a nice little place."

"How would your wife feel about it?"

"You don't have to worry about her. Why don't you try to think of a good location. I would like to have you where I could come to you after work. I want to be able to get away from Hiratsuka and Fujisawa, and Atsugi. I've been thinking maybe we could find a place near Chigasaki, right in the middle of them."

"I'll see if I can think of something," said Eiko, taking the warm saké from the kettle.

The next morning, the fifth of January, Shida went first to the plant at Hiratsuka, and a short time later, on to the plant at Atsugi. Work had already begun and the men were busy butchering and boning pork. Long ago they had bought whole porks in the meat markets of Tokyo and Yokohama, but now they only bought limbs and parts of the hog. Most of the meat was imported from Taiwan in refrigerated containers. Other kinds of meat, principally mutton and rabbit, were used for making sausage. Along with using machines to make meat processing easier, the current trend was to use any kind of meat whatsoever. It was said that some ham companies even used dog meat in their sausage, but the Shida Ham Company never did that. There was nothing particularly wrong in mixing dog meat with the ham. After all, horsemeat was regularly added. But the Shidas chose not to use dog meat in the same spirit that moved them to continue the old-fashioned process of smoking meat with beech chips.

Next to the butchering room, workers were pulling from vats the cuts of meat that had been cured and pickled during the holiday season. These cuts were carried to another room where they were wrapped in casings, and then taken to the smokehouse, where they were electronically smoked and made into ham.

The brick smokehouse was set apart from the rest of the plant. When Shida went there to inspect, he found a worker hanging two hams from the ceiling. "Is that a special order?" he asked.

"The boss ordered it," replied the worker.

"But my father should have already gotten a couple of smoked hams before the holidays began."

"He said he was planning to give them as presents," the worker replied.

Shida wondered to whom his father would be giving presents this early in the new year. As he gazed at the hams, he began to imagine what his wife would look like smoking there. This thought came to him unbidden, but the vision did not seem disagreeable. He could imagine her being finely ground by the grinding machine, mixed with spices and seasonings, and being kneaded into sausage. He no longer felt any attachment for his wife, only bitterness. A physical pain would let up, in time, but this emotional pain endured and dragged its victim on and on through a useless, pessimistic life.

Returning to his office, Shida paused to take stock of himself and realized such thoughts were unhealthy. Spending the holidays with Eiko should have revived his spirits, but it was clear that he still felt bitter. He had tried to destroy the garden Kase built, and while he was doing it had been able to forget his pain, but the respite was only temporary.

The telephone rang and his receptionist informed him that Mr. Kawada was on the line.

"Hello. How did things turn out with your garden?" came Kawada's voice.

"My garden?" Only then did Shida recall that Kawada had been the one who introduced him to Kase.

"Everything ought to be in place by now. When the weather gets a little warmer would you mind if I come by and take some photographs?"

"Photographs of the garden?"

"Of course photographs of the garden. I'd also like to take some of the house."

"I can't let you do that."

"You can't? What do you mean, you can't? I came to see it when it was first completed; it is quite a nice garden. It's considered one of Mr. Kase's recent masterpieces, that garden of yours."

Now that he mentioned it, Shida recalled that Kawada had come to see the garden before. He remembered him saying he wanted to come and take photos after the garden had had a chance to grow in a bit.

"I just can't let you do that."

"What's wrong with just taking a few pictures?"

"Have you talked to Kase about it?"

"It's always been understood between Kase and me that I'd be taking some photos."

"That's what you say, but you should talk to Kase again."

"Why? Did something happen between you and Kase?"

"No. Nothing. I'm busy, I have to hang up now."

Shida hung up the phone. He was upset. He did not have anything against Kawada, but he could not bear the thought of meeting him now. He decided that perhaps the best thing would be to sell the house and garden and be rid of them completely.

On the morning of January second when her husband had left the house, Mizue knew he would not return that night, but she had not imagined he would still not be home by the fifth. It had been a cold holiday season. No one had come to visit them. She wondered if Kase was spending this holiday season in a hotel as usual. When she had met him on the twenty-sixth, she had forgotten to ask what his plans were.

It seemed strange at New Year's time not to have the whole family together. It must have seemed strange to the children and to Momoko as well, to have the father of the house leave and not return.

There had been no rain for some time, and the garden was dry and dusty. How like her relationship with her husband.

Shida returned home after six o'clock that evening. Tonight as usual there was no discussion of where he had been.

"Would it be asking too much for you not to be away from home for days on end like this?" asked Mizue, but Shida did not bother to reply. He went through the New Year's greeting cards that had arrived during his absence, looking at each one carefully.

"It makes things awkward for the children and Momoko."

"It makes things awkward for you."

"That's right."

"You certainly look out for yourself."

"That's right, I do. But I still don't think it's fair to get the children involved in this."

"The children have no idea what is going on."

"They certainly think it odd for their father to leave home for days at a time during the New Year's holiday."

"Their father is busy as usual. Tell them that. I don't enjoy it very much, having to be in the same room with you. How can you have the nerve to ask me to come back every night and be with you?"

"I'm begging you to do it, even if it means coming home late. I don't mind as long as you come home."

"I'll see what I can do."

Presently Shida took the New Year's cards and went into the family room. Mizue thought that he had probably gone to write replies. She gazed at the cushion her husband had been sitting on. Such composure meant he must have taken up with another woman. In mid-November, on the way home after meeting Kase at the hotel in Shinagawa, she had wondered if she would feel jealous if her husband found someone else. Now that he was actually staying away from home, she found she felt nothing. She did not know for sure that he had another woman. In fact, she did not even care enough to feel suspicious.

She had not had a man since the twenty-sixth of December; this was the tenth day. She would not have minded even having her husband, but she did not really expect that. She decided that after the seventh of January, when the children returned to school, she would arrange to meet Kase again. She had no grounds for complaint if her husband paid her no attention. But her life was bitter as the days passed, and she found no comfort.

3

On the afternoon of January third, as Tamiko prepared to return home, Kase had told her he planned to be at his apartment until the tenth. On the eighth he received a phone call from Tamiko saying she would come to visit the following day and planned to spend the night. Kase had been asked to build a garden for a family in Zushi, a town on the other side of Kamakura. They owned a dry goods store at Nihonbashi in Tokyo and had come to Kase with their request on the twenty-seventh of December. The following day Kase had gone to Zushi to see their new home. The house was a single-story traditional Japanese-style dwelling of 2,500 square feet surrounded by a garden about four times that size. The head of the household appeared to be in his sixties and apparently was a collector of tea bowls. On the east side of the property were his personal quarters, and he asked that a dry landscape garden be built facing it. The property adjoined a pine forest. Kase thought he could keep the garden from looking too spare by building a wall and using the pine forest as part of the background view. Just to be sure he asked if a dry landscape garden wouldn't appear too stark from the house, but the owner said it would be fine. On the west side was a tea house, and Kase would have to put in a tea garden there.

Kase had just completed drawing plans for this garden.

Tamiko arrived before ten o'clock on the ninth. Kase had just awakened and was smoking the first cigarette of the day. "Don't you think you're ridiculously early?" he asked. He was surprised to see her.

"Mother and Father took my daughter and went off to Narita for the night. I don't suppose you've eaten yet?" Tamiko took a wrapped package out of a paper sack.

"Yesterday was the last day for getting meals sent in from the restaurant, so I was just thinking of going out for breakfast."

"I'm going to fix breakfast for you. I've brought some fish, yellowtail."

"Are there winter yellowtail available?"

"Apparently the fishermen set up their nets two days ago."

"Well, this is a real treat. It's been a long time since I had raw fish for breakfast."

Ever since he was a boy Kase had loved the winter yellowtail from Odawara. At his home there, whenever it was winter yellowtail season, his family would go to the market and buy a whole fish. They would chop it up and mix it with a generous amount of wild horseradish to make a savory dish they never grew tired of eating, even when they had it three meals in succession. The waste parts of the fish were boiled with round slices of daikon radish to give it a marvelous flavor. Kase had been away too long from life with such wholesome food. Tamiko had also brought along two large, wild horseradishes.

Mizue arrived just as Kase and Tamiko were eating the chopped fish.

When the buzzer rang Tamiko put down her chopsticks and went to the door. She returned a few moments later with a puzzled look on her face.

"It's that Mrs. Shida I saw here once before."

Kase told her that since they were eating in the living room, they should invite her into the study. He stopped eating and got up from the table. Tamiko went to prepare tea.

When Kase went to the study, Mizue explained that she had called his office and been told he was home today.

"I've been asked to build a garden at a house in Zushi. I've been drawing the plans for it here," Kase said.

"Oh, if I'm in the way here . . ."

"No, not at all. Why do you say that?"

"Well, if it's all right then," said Mizue. She looked uncertain.

"How are things at home?"

"They keep getting worse. Couldn't we go out?" Mizue looked at the floor. "I can't just turn around and go home. Not today."

"Let's go out, then." Kase left the study and called into the living room, "Tami, we're going out for a little bit." Then he went to the bedroom to get his overcoat.

Mizue had gone out into the corridor ahead of him. As Kase was putting on his shoes, Tamiko asked what he would like for dinner.

"Anything will be fine. I never complain when I have a chance to eat your cooking."

As they left the building, Kase took stock of his position, caught as he was between two women. As he walked down the hill with Mizue, he saw himself and Mizue as utterly desolate, a man and a woman walking through a desolate landscape. Mizue walked as one who wandered aimlessly.

"Are things really that bad for you?" he asked.

"I have no place to live. Every day I keep telling myself that. I have no place to live. It may sound strange to hear me say this, but that's the way I feel. I don't know if he has another woman or not, but during the holidays he left home on the second and didn't return until the fifth." Mizue spoke simply. "But even if I tell you these things, there is nothing you can do."

That's right, thought Kase, listening calmly to what Mizue was saying. There is nothing I can do.

"If you can leave your family," he said aloud, "You can come live with me."

But, thought Mizue, I don't see much hope with Kase either. She could not say this aloud.

There were several hotels lined up near the west entrance of Yokohama Station. As they reached the bottom of the hill Kase decided they would have to go to one of them.

Later, on the train going home, Mizue wondered if her violent emotional response was due to jealousy. Kase had called the other woman by the intimate name "Tami." Last time he had said she was the daughter of one of his relatives, but the casual way she made herself at home in Kase's apartment indicated something else. She did not, however, question Kase about this Tami. She had believed him before, but now she did not. At the hotel, as Kase took her body in his arms, she was overcome by a wave of jealousy. The fury of her feelings surprised even her. Mizue had thought she alone could comprehend the spiritual and emotional vision of this garden builder, but Tami's devotion indicated that she had completely lost her head over him. Something that had belonged to Mizue exclusively had suddenly been snatched away. But she had a husband and children of her own; what was it she was being deprived of? Mizue did not feel she was merely being selfish. Tami could not possibly fully understand Kase, the artist. She decided to ask him about this the next time they met.

4

On the eighteenth of January Kase began work on the garden at Zushi. To separate his property from the adjoining land, the owner wanted a traditional clay wall, topped with tiles in the style called Aburabei. Kase had not built such a wall in a long while; it would require time and patience. First he would have to build a wall of stone, tiles, and clay; next he would top the wall with tiles, and finally he would have to finish the surface with stucco. An old treatise on garden making says this about constructing such a wall:

Eight parts lime, four parts salt, and one part clay. Mix these ingredients, pound them in a mortar, allow to dry for one day, then again pound finely in a mortar. To this mixture add five parts oil, two parts salt, and three parts water. Pound with a pestle and after it reaches a smooth consistency, pound further with a smaller pestle.

No one knew who thought up this recipe, but Kase had found the mixture worked well. The compound could be used not only for making walls but also for making a hard surface on the ground if the amount of lime was reduced by half and white sand was used to make up the difference. Kase wondered if this wasn't what they used in the garden at the Shisendo temple in Kyoto. The best known example of the Aburabei-style wall was the one around the rock garden at the Ryoanji.

Kase planned a plain Aburabei wall along the north side of the garden; on the other three sides he would make a low mound of earth and plant a hedge with the Aburabei running in front of it. That way, when looking from the garden, the hedge would be visible beyond the wall. Since the front of the property was high and the garden itself was lower, it formed its own secluded world. Here he was not able to exploit the surrounding natural landscape as he had at the home of the painter in Yamagata, where the mountains and the river had created a setting for the garden. Here, the safest course was one of isolation. It was not an extravagant garden, but it had elegance and good taste. Kase designed it with the owner's remaining years in mind.

First Kase would have to bring in the stones for the garden. Then he would build the foundations for the earthen wall. While the wall was drying, he would put in the hedge. Finally, he would apply the stucco surface on the wall. Since the surrounding areas were all raised, it would be necessary to cut a channel for the rain that would naturally flow from the gar-den toward the house. He would pave this stream channel with stone and design it so that it would also carry away the runoff from the roof of the house.

The problem was the dry landscape on the east side. Kase had in mind something like the garden at the Tofukuji, but was afraid it might end up having the same crude shallowness as that design. It was inevitable now that he swing back and forth between Mizue and Tamiko. Just as he had completed the drawings for this garden, both women had shown up at his apartment. That day, as he parted from Mizue at Yokohama Station and returned to Hodogaya, he had associated Mizue with the stones of the dry landscape garden, and Tamiko with the tea garden on the west side. Such an association was inescapable. Both the stone and tea gardens had to be isolated from the main garden. The dry landscape was cut off by the Aburabei wall, and the tea garden could be isolated by the shrubbery.

Eight years ago, when he had built a garden in Kamakura, Kase had used tempura oil for an Aburabei wall with disastrous results. He had tried again and successfully used mustard seed oil, the sort used in making tofu. The old manuals had not specified the kind of oil to be used. Later he had learned that a mixture of mustard seed oil and sesame seed oil would make a harder wall.

Once he began work on the garden he did not rest even on weekends, and only took a holiday when it rained.

One afternoon, after he had worked with his two students building the core of the earthen wall, Kase went to the stone yard at Fujisawa to order stone lanterns. He always ordered his lanterns there. There was an old book published in 1798 called *Musoryu Jitei*, or "Principles of Muso-style Gardens," which, despite its name, had not of course actually been written by the famous medieval Zen priest and garden designer Muso Soseki. No doubt it had been written by some lover of classical elegance who had attached Muso's name to his own book. Kase was nevertheless interested in the book's illustrations of unusually shaped stone lanterns, and he had re-interpreted them in modern ways. The old stone lanterns' designs—each one named after a famous tea master—would be appreciated by any cultured person. Kase planned to put a Shuko-style lantern at the entrance to the tea garden at Zushi, and an Enshu-style lantern just next to the tea house. The Shuko lantern would be about a foot square and would stand more than forty inches high with the capstone above that. Forthright and simple, its shape was strong. The Enshu lantern had an unusual design and was composed of five layers of stone. He chose one less than twenty inches tall.

Kase always had his stone lanterns made of red-tinted granite. Most stone yards used a chemical compound to color the granite, but Kase did the work himself, preserving the methods found in the ancient books on gardening. It was a lot of work. He would take butterburs, roots and all, chop and mix them with water, then pound them in a mortar to extract their fluid. This liquid was then boiled with chimney soot, and mixed with persimmon juice. When this compound was brushed on a stone, the result was a quality of restrained elegance or *shibumi*. Using chemicals to tint the stone could never achieve this effect, just as the shades of blue produced by natural indigo are very different from those produced by chemical dyes. The special butterburs Kase used were found on the slopes of the mountain range bordering the coast of the Miura Peninsula south of Kamakura. If these plants were not available, there were a couple of other plants whose roots could be used to obtain the same color. Avoiding chemical dyes in tinting the stones was one more element in Kase's struggle against the commonplace.

Kase gave his specifications for the lanterns to the owner of the stone yard and asked that they be ready by the end of March. Then, leaving his truck there, he walked a hundred yards or so to a small Chinese restaurant for lunch.

Kase sat down at a table, ordered a bowl of noodles, and then waited, smoking a cigarette. Happening to look up, he saw, in a seat in front of him, the profile of Eiji Shida. Shida was eating the same kind of noodles Kase had ordered. He thought such a meeting a curious coincidence, but he was not about to get up and leave. It occurred to Kase that the home office of the Shida Ham Company must be in this neighborhood.

Presently Kase's noodles were served. By that time Shida had finished his meal and was smoking a cigarette. Kase kept an eye on Shida as he ate his noodles and saw him finish the cigarette and stand up. At that moment Shida became aware of Kase and their eyes met. Shida said nothing, but walked to the door, paid his bill, and left. Though Kase did not turn to watch, he could feel Shida's movements through his back. Kase did not blame Shida for feeling the way he did. His thoughts went back to Mizue's last visit to Hodogaya and his impression that she was drifting aimlessly now. Toward the end of spring nearly a year ago, on his way to meet Emiko at a hotel, he had wondered if Mizue would be able to cleanse him of the filth he felt. But instead, his life had only gotten worse. He still considered

Mizue indispensable to him. And yet he felt he had caused her to lose too much. He had paralyzed her, in a sense. If only it were nothing more than a physical relationship, he thought. But as it is, neither of us can be saved.

When he finished eating and went out, Shida was waiting for him. "I had intended to have a few words with you, but after thinking it over, I have decided that I have nothing to say to a person like you. I think you're disgusting." Shida spit out the words and, turning his back on Kase, walked away.

As Shida walked away his back seemed to suggest the contrast between the two men; it was the garden that separated them. There was nothing for them to talk about.

Back in Zushi, Kase found his friend Kawada from the publishing company waiting for him. A week earlier he had received a phone call from Kawada and they had arranged to meet today.

"Some time ago you showed me the drawings for this garden. It looks as though it will turn out very well," said Kawada.

"Well, I wonder. It's hard to tell how a garden is going to turn out before it is finished. As I told you on the phone the other day, I think it would be better if you do not photograph Shida's garden after all."

"Why? Did something happen between you and Shida?"

"No, not really. Some little thing came up and we quarreled. Shida got mad and tore up the garden."

"Tore up the garden? What did you quarrel about?"

"It was nothing really. It happens all the time, you know. Something came up and before we knew it, we were quarreling."

"He's such a calm person, I can't believe he would fight with anyone. But tell me, what did he do to the garden?"

"I don't know. I haven't seen it. He just phoned and said he had torn it up and that he didn't want to see me there again."

Kase felt compelled to make something up. He had seen Shida's back as symbolic of the contrast between them, and it was painful for Kase too.

He took Kawada out to the main street for a cup of coffee and there they parted.

5

Her husband was fine. He had to be keeping a mistress, but since all this had begun, he had kept himself remote from Mizue. She realized this was not because of Kase. Her feeling of estrangement from her husband had been growing ever since the year she lost all three members of her family. She still had a commitment to the children. No matter how often she reflected on this problem, Mizue could not simply put the children aside and pretend they did not exist. It made no difference how pure her relationship with Kase was.

Shida had gotten into the habit of staying away from home almost every other night. As usual Mizue did not question him and he did not explain. They still slept in the same room, but once nightfall came, they were strangers. It did not seem possible they could go on living this way. It was hard to imagine what sort of woman her husband was keeping, since he had never fooled around. But she knew that he lived his life outside the home now, and when he did return, he did not need his wife.

On the morning of the twenty-fourth, Mizue saw the children off to school, and then set out for Zushi.

Kase was staying at a hotel on the coast near Zushi and commuting to the garden site from there. It was an old wooden hotel and the floors creaked as Mizue walked along the corridors. Kase's room was on the ground floor at the far eastern side of the building.

Kase had said it was too much trouble to go all the way back to Hodogaya every evening, and by staying at the hotel in Zushi he could visit the garden several times a day. Papers were spread all over his desk, probably the manuscript of the book on garden building he was writing. Outside his window was a yellowed lawn and beyond that spread the sea itself.

"Is Tamiko staying here with you?"

"Tami? Her child is ill. I haven't seen her since the last time you visited me."

"Have you known her longer than you've known me?" asked Mizue, gazing out at the sea.

"Her husband died and she has gone home to live with her parents."

"You don't seem very sympathetic toward her. Does she realize you can't give her any hope for the future?"

"I never thought about that very much. I did tell you, though, that if you will leave your family, you are welcome to come live with me."

"Yes, but you know I can't leave my family, so it really doesn't mean anything when you say that." Mizue moved away from the window and sat in a chair.

"You shouldn't think that way. I once said I could demonstrate our love to Shida. I actually went to him once and asked him to give you to me."

"I'm sorry. I'm not quite myself."

There was no point going over and over the same ground.

Right now Kase was preoccupied with the problem of placing the stones in the dry landscape garden he was building. If the vertical stones blended smoothly with the surroundings, the garden might perhaps achieve a sense of great, open expanse. The garden at the Tofukuji looked unrefined to Kase; it lacked the serenity found in the garden at the Shodenji in Kyoto, with its luxuriant clumps of azalea and borrowed view of Mount Hiei. The Tofukuji garden inspired repulsion and empathy, two emotions that Kase, as a gardener, knew quite well. Kase did not build gardens in the Zen tradition. What he could build were dry landscapes that simply evoked mountains and streams, and he so far had never gone beyond this. This time, however, it seemed he might go further, and it frightened him. If the stones should happen to express Mizue's unrestrained sensuality, what would he do then? Looking at the garden of the Tofukuji with a critical eye, it seemed to float loose from its surroundings, revealing the builder's selfish motives. Kase felt it was a garden builder's responsibility to never create a garden that made the viewer aware of what he was thinking. He was worried that the dry landscape he was now building would turn out looking contrived. Even if the tea garden on the west side of the property were to neutralize this effect, the east side of the garden might still attract attention.

"You are a stone," said Kase, smoking a cigarette after they had made love.

"I think you are the stone," replied Mizue without opening her eyes.

"No, I'm more like the wind. I could never be a stone."

"Is it because you sweep over a woman like the wind and pass on? Perhaps you are the wind."

Mizue recalled the time she had talked to Kase at the eel restaurant in Oiso. At that time she had the impression that he was like the wind blowing among the stones on the side of a barren mountain. This man has placed countless numbers of stones; I wonder if he can do anything more than pass over them, she thought. If only it were possible, I would live with him, and when he went to some remote place to build a garden, I would go with him and cook for him, and when he was at home in his study, I would be in the kitchen preparing food. That was Mizue's fantasy.

"Would you say that this Tamiko is indispensable to you?"

"Why do you ask?"

"Don't you think it's cruel to attract a woman like her? She doesn't really understand you."

"Oh, I guess that's one way to look at it."

"You know as well as I do that you don't want to take just anything that comes along. Please leave her."

"It would be easy enough to leave her; I haven't promised her anything. I want you to wait until I have completed the garden I'm building here in Zushi. Then will you leave Hadano and come live with me?"

"Will you definitely leave Tamiko once you've finished the garden?"

"Yes, I believe I will."

"Then I will leave Hadano and come live with you."

"Are you sure you're prepared to make such a promise?"

"To go on living there is no better than being dead."

"Will you be able to leave your children?"

"Please don't ask me. I'm sure it will be a difficult thing to do and I will have regrets afterward, but when the time comes, I'll be able to do it."

Her husband was away from home every day now. There was no question he was abandoning his family. Mizue understood that he did not have much interest in coming home to her and the children and to the garden he himself had destroyed. Mizue believed their family life had been destroyed too and that they were merely playing out the final scenes in whatever form they might take. Two days ago in the afternoon her husband had returned home with a real estate agent. As soon as the agent showed up to make an estimate of the value of the house and the land, Mizue realized the end had come.

6

From Hadano Shida could never see Mount Tanzawa, but he could sense that he was at the foot of a huge mountain range. Going back and forth by car between Hadano and Atsugi on Highway 246, he ran along the foot of the mountains, unable to see the whole Tanzawa massif. But from Hiratsuka, he got a good view of the mountains. When Shida got up in the morning and went out on the veranda, the Tanzawa range stood clearly etched against the morning sky, its ridgeline buried in snow; in the evening the slopes were dyed by the western sun, and when at last the sun was gone, they loomed in silhouette against the sky.

Shida had not given much thought to what he might do after he sold his house in Hadano, but he was certain that he would leave the slopes of these mountains. He might rent a place in Atsugi, or perhaps build another house somewhere. For some time he had hesitated to sell the house because it had been designed especially for him, incorporating the surrounding landscape into the plan. But once he decided to sell, he had no misgivings.

From Hiratsuka, Shida gazed at Mount Tanzawa and seemed to recognize his own ruined home on the slopes of the mountain. He could not actually see his house, of course, but every time he went out onto the veranda he could envision the ruins of his family, ruins that could never be rebuilt. The end of February would soon be upon them.

On nights Shida spent with her, Eiko did not go to work at the hot springs resort. She had looked for a small shop of some sort, as Shida had suggested, and had found several, but none was just what she had in mind. Shida was also looking, as he mentioned, but also at Ofuna and at Kamakura. If it were simply a matter of renting a shop and turning it over to her, there were a number of such properties available, but Shida also wanted a place with living quarters.

It was Sunday morning. As Shida drank his tea, he reminded Eiko that

145

she was supposed to return to her home in Udoko the following day.

"But I really don't have to go home."

"Why not?"

"I feel guilty about going home and leaving you alone every week."

"You don't have to worry. You know, what I would really like to do is retire to the country with you and spend the rest of my life making handmade paper."

"It's terrible to hear you say something like that. You're just getting into your best working years, aren't you?"

Eiko had heard all about Mizue from Shida. He had told her then that he had never supposed his relationship with her would become such a consolation to him.

"But I also feel sorry for your wife. Don't you think it's hard for her too?"

"No. I have no sympathy for her."

Eiko had felt gentle sympathy for Shida, knowing that his family had been very important to him, and that his wounds were deep.

Shida finished his tea and went out onto the veranda smoking a cigarette. The Tanzawa massif presented its snow-covered peaks to him. He had not been back to Hadano since Friday. The massif consisted of three main peaks: Oyama, Sannoto, and Togatake. As a youth he had often hiked along those mountain ridges. One autumn on a hike from Sannoto, he had encountered a great storm of wind and rain and spent two days shut up in a small wayside shrine on Togatake.

Walking back into the room, he compared his life now with how things had been in the past. He wondered if there was some way to regain the uncomplicated emotional freshness he had known hiking in the mountains.

Eiko came in from the kitchen where she had been tidying up and asked, "Wouldn't it be better if you went home today?"

"I'll go home tomorrow."

Shida continued to stay with Eiko even though he was afraid his continued absence from home would be bad for his children.

Even now Mizue continued to have flowers delivered every Monday from the nearby flower farm. On this Sunday morning, however, she finished breakfast and set out for the farm herself.

She found the wife of the eldest son in the greenhouse. "It's a day early, but I wonder if you have any flowers available?" she called out from the doorway.

"Oh, Mrs. Shida, please come in. I'm just gathering some thistles."

"Thistles are pretty. I like them," said Mizue, entering the greenhouse and walking to where the wife stood. The woman held a basket filled with beautiful flowers. They were quite unlike the wild thistles that merely grow and bloom in season.

"I think I would like to have about ten." Mizue also took twenty Japanese narcissus. Returning home with her bundle of flowers, she found her son, Eiichi, in the living room drinking tea.

"Dad always used to take us out to eat on Sundays, but it seems like he's never home anymore." Eiichi sounded quite grown up when he looked at Mizue and spoke this way.

"I don't like to hear you talk that way about your father." Even as she rebuked the child, Mizue felt that somewhere deep within him, somewhere that could not be seen, there was already a wound. It would only be a matter of time until this wound became apparent to everyone.

Mizue spread a figured mat in the hallway. As she arranged the flowers, she made up her mind to meet Kase tomorrow. The real question for Mizue was whether or not she could really make a new start with Kase. She had not changed her mind about going to him. Although there were sides of Kase's character she still did not understand, as things stood now, she had no other place to go.

Mizue passed the hours with nothing to do. Finally, in the afternoon she took Momoko with her shopping. Even if her husband did not come home, she still had to make dinner. She had never come right out and said, "Oh well, I don't expect him home this evening." Besides, it was Mizue's nature to make all the right preparations.

After they had finished shopping and returned home, they found a large black car parked in front of the gate. It belonged to the real estate agent from Odawara. Since the end of January this car had arrived from time to time bringing various potential buyers.

The agent and his clients were waiting for Mizue in the living room. The clients greeted Mizue saying that since she had been out when they arrived, they had gone ahead and shown the house. The client produced his calling card and placed it before Mizue. The card indicated that he was the president of the Yamazaki Container Manufacturing Company, which produced cardboard boxes.

"Your son told us your husband is away on business today," said the agent.

"That's right. If you wish to communicate with him, you can reach him at his office tomorrow."

Mizue could not be sure whether or not the children really believed Shida was away on business, but she remembered Eiichi's remark that his father was never at home anymore.

After a time the visitors got up to go. In the entry hall as they were leaving, the real estate agent whispered to Mizue that he thought these people were serious about buying the house. As she saw the guests to their car and watched them drive off, Mizue had an empty feeling that these people might indeed decide to take the home. Her husband hadn't told her he was definitely going to sell it.

7

Kase was smoking the first cigarette of the day in bed. The air in the room felt heavy and sultry. "It must be raining," thought Kase as he got up and opened the curtains. Apparently it had been raining for some time. There were puddles of water in the courtyard of the hotel. Mist was rising like smoke over the ocean.

He called room service to order breakfast and went into the bathroom.

Emerging from the shower, he found the table set with coffee and plates of toast. It occurred to him that if the rain kept up for several days, he would be able to finish his manuscript. As he was drinking his coffee, he got a telephone call from one of his student helpers. It was raining in Tokyo and the student wondered what the weather was like in Zushi. When Kase replied that it was raining there too, the student said he would take the opportunity to go to school for a change.

Kase had a feeling that either Mizue or Tamiko would come see him today. As he looked out over the smoky, rain-drenched sea, his mind thought back over the two women and how their bodies differed. It had been almost half a month since Mizue had been to see him. Tamiko had come the previous Sunday. If he mixed eight parts lime, four parts salt, and one part clay, then what mixture of mustard seed oil and sesame would be best? Sunday he had been gazing at Tamiko's peach-colored cleft when he noticed a pale yellow mucus flowing from it. He had never seen anything like this before and it made him uneasy. There is a cactus called Moonlight Maiden, with a large, round, pure white flower which blooms on summer evenings. It gives off a pungent fragrance for a few hours and then withers away. Kase had once seen this flower in November. He had picked it, thinking it would bloom that night. Sure enough, the blossom began to open around nine o'clock, giving off its perfume until the room was filled with its fragrance. The flower had a complex arrangement of pistils and stamens, and it was impossible to tell from exactly where the fragrance was coming. Just as the blossom's aroma began to fade, the blossom itself began to wither and die. Kase viewed Tamiko's rich fluid in the same way. It almost looked like the juice that flows from a fish's stomach when it is cut open. He did not suppose she would know even if he asked her what it was. It must be an essential fluid of life. He'd never seen it coming out of Mizue's body. What mixture of mustard seed oil and sesame oil should he use? In order to build an Aburabei wall, the garden builder's spirit must fully penetrate the spirit of his creation.

Mizue arrived shortly before eleven. Kase was surprised to see her wearing Western clothes.

"Has Tamiko been here since the last time I was here? I don't like to ask such questions, but it has been bothering me," said Mizue, seating herself in a chair.

"She's been here," replied Kase without evasion.

"You said it would be easy to break with her, but if she refused to leave you, what would you do then?"

"I guess I never really thought it out before."

"You told me you had not made any promises or commitments to her, but a woman never pays attention to that sort of thing anyway. If you are going to break with her, I think it would be better if you did it soon."

Mizue had already told Kase that her husband was in the process of selling the house. She told him now about the clients the real estate agent had brought the previous afternoon. There was a real possibility that the house would soon be sold. When that happened, she said, she would leave her family and come to him.

"As I told you, you'll always be welcome here."

"And if I do that, what will you do with Tamiko?"

"I'll break with her."

"Will you really? I wonder. She is younger and prettier than I am, and I wonder if you will really break with her."

"I promise."

It once would have been quite easy for him to break with Tamiko. And not just with Tamiko; with all the women he had known, he had only to think about breaking up with them and he could do it. Yet Kase now found that Tamiko was just as necessary to him as Mizue. Once a week Tamiko came seeking him quietly, passed the time in the elegant style of old, and then went away. Such a woman was just like a tea garden. Kase's response to Tamiko's body contrasted sharply to the unrestrained passion of his encounters with Mizue. Tamiko was necessary now to Kase.

He did not see any trace of a thick, yellow fluid coming out of Mizue's body. She was able to make love with abandon, and yet there was something about her that Kase could not understand.

"You truly are a stone," said Kase.

"You're just repeating what you said before. All I want is to be with you, to make miso soup for you and nothing more."

"That may be so. But you're still a stone. All I am is the wind."

"You're trying to put me off, to get rid of me."

Mizue envisioned the wind blowing among the stones on the side of a barren mountain. That was the force she always felt with Kase. Where did this wind come from, where did it go? Did it only exist now to caress her skin? After it left her, did it exist at all, did it leave nothing behind? When she had surrendered her body to Kase before, she had felt the wick of her existence being extinguished; now all she felt was uneasiness.

Why was it that after making love with Kase she always remembered that terrible year when all the members of her family died?

It was past one o'clock by the time Mizue felt restored enough to leave the hotel. In the taxi back to the station she watched rain streaming against the windows. She thought idly that she might be even more unhappy if she went to live with Kase.

There was a knock at the door ten minutes after Mizue had left.

"Come in, the door's open," called Kase from the bed. He thought it must be the maid, but it was Tamiko who entered the room.

"Oh, Tami, it's you." It must be on account of the rain, he thought.

"I arrived here about noon, but the man at the front desk told me, so I went to the dining room and had lunch. What else could I do?"

"I'm sorry. That must have been very unpleasant for you."

It seemed outrageous, for her to have lunch in the dining room waiting for her lover who was with another woman. From the bed Kase looked at Tamiko and recalled that Mizue had asked him what he would do if Tamiko said she would not leave him.

Weekends were busy, but the rest of the time the hotel was mostly empty. The clerk at the front desk knew that Kase had two women visiting him regularly.

Kase showered once again.

"I guess I'll just go home." Tamiko sat in a chair staring down at her knees. She wore a black pantsuit. It looked good on her.

"Have I made you feel bad?" Kase sat on the edge of the bed with a a bath towel around his waist.

"No, not really. It's just that you were in love with that other woman before I came along. I guess there is nothing I can do about it."

"But I've known you far longer than I've known her. You can think of it that way too." Kase realized it must be unpleasant for her to climb into a bed that another woman had just occupied. Since Mizue, like Tamiko, always straightened up before she left, the room was in order. Emiko had been the sort of woman who filled the wastebaskets with trash, then went off and left them. In Kase's experience there had been many women like Emiko, women who dyed their hair, painted their nails, and wore wigs.

"I can't stand it! Yusaku, I can't stand it!" Tears came to Tamiko's eyes.

Kase dressed and went to the telephone to order a bottle of white wine. A short time later a bell boy arrived with the wine.

"Drink some of this," Kase told Tamiko, "and you'll feel better."

He filled two glasses and put one in Tamiko's hand. It occurred to Kase now that if he took Mizue as his mate he would exist as a garden builder and artist, and if he chose Tamiko he would exist as a man. Both women were undeniably feminine. Now, for the first time, Kase could see that he was standing at a crossroads. He was not afraid of the two women. He reflected, rather, with something like regret, that it was he who had entangled the two of them. Certainly Mizue was in a position from which she could not withdraw.

Tamiko left the hotel and went out into the rain. She wondered why things had turned out this way. Up to this point she had not thought much about Mizue Shida. She had considered her nothing more than a married woman playing at adultery. As soon as the desk clerk told her Kase had a woman guest, she knew it was Mizue. She had gone to the dining room and eaten a light lunch, and suddenly her thoughts went back to her and Kase's earlier meeting on January ninth. As she had prepared the winter yellowtail, she had thought about Mizue's arrival. Yusaku had gone out with her and returned three hours later. She had thought at the time that they had probably gone to a hotel somewhere. Tamiko had been unhappy, but she had not really felt any jealousy then. She had reminded herself that the other woman had established herself first as Kase's lover.

But today, as she was eating lunch, she could not help thinking that the two of them were in his room in bed together. She wondered if he was doing the same things with this other woman that he did with her. Soon her feelings were in disarray, but she couldn't burst into the room while the two were there. She called to mind Kase's face and remembered him telling her he could make no promises. She told herself to keep her feelings under control.

Tamiko had finished eating, taken a seat in the lobby, and had a cup of coffee while she waited. Half an hour later, Mizue had appeared in the lobby and climbed into a taxi. The desk clerk had then come to Tamiko and informed her that the other woman had left. He was middle-aged, and Tamiko felt embarrassed that she had come to visit a man at a hotel. Tamiko bowed and thanked him, but remained for a time sitting in the chair.

The full force of her jealousy did not come to Tamiko until she entered the room and saw Kase lying in bed.

Rain blew against the windows of the taxi. Today for the first time Tamiko was aware her body had matured, but whether her awareness came from her repeated meetings with Kase, or from her jealousy, she could not be sure. In the midst of confusion and jealousy she was encountering a world she had never known before. After making love to Kase, she had clearly felt herself full and complete. Kase had said he could promise her nothing, but she felt that was unreasonable. I want to see him, she thought, even if I cannot live with him. She had never thought it possible for a man and a woman to be so inseparable.

8

The house at Hadano was sold and the promissory note agreed upon. One-third of the price was paid at the time the note was signed, and the rest would be paid a month later when the house was vacated and turned over to the new owner.

As he received the check and signed the receipt, Shida felt completely drained. He wondered why he had ever bothered to build this house. When it was under construction, he remembered, he had come to the site virtually every day.

After the real estate agent and his client left, Shida called his wife to him and told her he had sold the house and that within the month they would have to rent a new house and move.

"I see," was all Mizue said.

"It's all the fault of that gardener. If you want to live with him, go ahead. Let him talk you into it. And if you decide you aren't going to leave, I suppose that's all right too. But neither you nor I will ever be the same again.

Nothing remains of our family except that we are living in the same house for the sake of the children." Shida left the room.

Soon Mizue heard the sound of the car starting up. She listened as it died away.

Her husband had returned from the plant shortly after noon, and almost immediately after him came the real estate agent and the president of the cardboard container company who had come earlier to see the house. By the time the sound of Shida's car had faded completely, Mizue felt she had no choice but to go live with Kase. But she could not be sure she would be able to leave when the time actually came. In the withered winter garden, the narcissus were blooming. Suddenly the unthinkable notion came to her that perhaps it had just been a temporary affair after all. No, surely it had been more than that.

Mizue called Momoko and asked her to have a taxi sent around. As she gazed at the desolate garden, she decided to visit the graves at Oiso.

At Hiratsuka she bought flowers.

After their marriage, Shida and Mizue had been careful to delineate their roles as man and woman, yet they had still felt they were two people joined as one. Why, then had things turned out this way? Mizue had the cab wait outside. As she walked through the gate into the temple compound, she thought back. All the years and months from the time of her marriage until today returned to her. She had no regrets over the way she had come to this point in her life.

The path to the cemetery was backed by a wooded mountain and the path itself was blown full of last year's fallen leaves. Blades of new spring grass were pushing up through them.

She placed the flowers in front of the grave markers and burned incense.

"I might leave Shida's house after all, and have my remains interred here with the rest of the family," Mizue murmured as she stood looking at the graves.

When Shida arrived at Atsugi, he went straight to a real estate agent and left his calling card, saying he would like to rent a house of moderate size. From there he went to the plant and phoned Eiko to say he would come to her place around six o'clock. He felt now that he only wanted to find a house to rent and leave Hadano as quickly as possible.

9

The garden he was building in Zushi needed a fair amount of dirt. Kase hauled it from Fujisawa where a hillside had collapsed. It was rich, black soil. He used a four-ton truck and hauled some thirty loads. When he dumped out the last load, three hibernating snakes emerged.

"I wonder if we brought a whole nest of them," said one of the students.

"When they're hibernating they can't move, can they?" asked the other.

Out in the cold midday, the snakes could barely move their bodies. Kase identified them as grass snakes.

"Shall we boil them?" asked one of the students, picking up one of the snakes. The snake seemed drowsy and could not even curl itself up; it just dangled from the student's hand.

"They wouldn't taste good. I feel sorry for them, being exposed like this. Let's bury them in the earthen wall."

"You mean give them a place where they can sleep permanently?"

"Yes."

"We'll do it after lunch."

They covered the three snakes with dirt.

They ate their lunch, as usual, in a Chinese restaurant on a busy street nearby. The students wolfed down their rice, noodles, and pot stickers.

After returning to the construction site they started to work, packing the dirt for the earthen Aburabei-style wall they had begun three days before. First they packed the inner face. They would finish that before going on to the outer face. Their formula of eight parts lime, four parts salt, and one part clay for the wall surface did not work at first. For the salt they had used crushed rock salt. Salt served as a hardening agent, just as it does when mixed with concrete and asphalt in road surfacing. Kase could not figure out how the people in ancient times had come up with the idea of using salt. Japan had no natural rock salt, and had to import all it needed from Korea or China. For the construction of an Aburabei wall, rock salt worked best.

Kase himself mixed the lime, salt, clay, and oil.

After lunch, the two students who had been hauling dirt were put to work building the wall. Counting Kase, that made a crew of six.

They did not use a mortar for mixing, as it said to do in the old manuals; rather, they mixed the ingredients with a shovel on an iron sheet. Any kind of clay would do if it was sticky, but red clay was best.

"Shall we seal all three snakes in together?" called one of the students from a distance. Kase stopped working with the shovel and looked in the direction of the voice. One of the students had all three snakes dangling from his hands.

"Bury them all separately."

The students didn't think about how cruel it was to seal up living things. The idea to bury the snakes in the wall had crossed Kase's mind suddenly. He had thought that the oil from the snake's bodies might seep out and stain a pattern on the surface. But that was an unscientific notion. The plaster surface of the wall was nearly an inch thick.

In the end, Kase sealed in the three snakes and smoothed over the wall surface with a trowel. He cautioned the students to say nothing of this to the owner of the house.

Kase finished the day's work, returned to his hotel, showered, and went out to eat. He always had dinner out. Today he went to his regular eating place.

As he sat drinking, his mind went back to the events of the afternoon and the three snakes sealed in the wall. He mused that what he had buried there was really Mizue, Tamiko, and himself. He could not begin work on the dry landscape garden or the tea garden until the Aburabei wall was finished. He could still envision Tamiko and Mizue seated on clusters of stones set in Moronobu's predatory garden. Even as he compared the two women, he could see no solution.

It has no stepping stones, but rather the appearance of a field.

Moronobu's words came back to Kase. As the third bottle of saké arrived, Kase wondered if drinking was all that was left. Like a broad, flat field with no stepping stones—how would he handle such a woman? Both the tea garden and the dry landscape garden were compatible with the flat garden; which way would he choose? He saw Tamiko as a tea garden and Mizue as a dry landscape. No matter how he considered the situation, he found himself at a fork in the road.

That night when he returned to the hotel he was drunker than he had ever been. Since the weather had already turned a good deal warmer, he decided to return to Hodogaya the next day and commute from there from then on. He also had to put in an appearance or two at the school where he taught.

10

In early January the fishermen had only caught a few yellowtail in their fixed nets, but in March there was a snowfall and once again they began catching the fish. As usual Tamiko's and Kase's families went in together on a single large fish which they split. Tamiko took the half that belonged to Kase's family and delivered it to their house.

"Oh, so they had you bring it, did they?" Kase's mother exclaimed.

It was evening. Tamiko wanted simply to deliver the fish and go home, but Kase's mother restrained her, insisting she stay and have a cup of tea first.

"I really have to get back and get supper started."

"Come now, you're not that busy. Have you seen Yusaku recently?"

"Yes." Tamiko knew her mother met Kase's mother at least every other day, and they always gossiped.

"Please take good care of him. If there is anything at all we can do to help out, we will."

Tamiko's mother had said the very same thing a few days earlier. "Don't split up with Yusaku," she had cautioned.

But Tamiko did not have to be told anything; she had become a full-grown woman by this man. Her eyes did not waver, but stayed focused right in front of her. Everything on the periphery was white, but straight ahead of her was burning red. She could not see what was in the depths of this fiery red, but she was convinced that if she walked straight into the middle of it, she would find something. Mizue Shida was in her field of vision, but Tamiko tried to drive her away to the white areas around the fringes. For now, Mizue existed as a deep, rich color. That was only because Mizue had established herself as Kase's lover first.

As she walked through the twilight streets on her way home, Tamiko knew she wanted to live with Yusaku.

Mizue gazed out at the withered garden.

A house had been found set back a short distance from a busy street in Atsugi, and in four days time they would move. Her husband had informed her of these arrangements the previous evening. He also said that in two days some of the younger employees from his company would arrive to do the packing. Shida had apparently told the people at work that he was moving because he had grown tired of the area.

Mizue, of course, was responsible for packing up all the things in the kitchen. Even if she were able to take this opportunity to leave the Shida household, she wanted to be certain that everything in the kitchen was in order. She decided that the next day she would have Momoko help her and begin packing the chinaware in boxes. But what were her own plans? That was the question. She had not made up her mind to leave the children. She had told Kase it was sad to see him seducing a young woman who did not really understand him, but it was possible that Kase did not mind. He was not the sort of man who treated women tenderly.

The trees in the garden cast long shadows in the slanting rays of the western sun. Shida had torn up the garden but it had not really been destroyed. This had been reconfirmed to Mizue over the past few days. The stones still served as Kase's eyes. Even the mysterious aspects of Kase's nature were now being revealed. Mizue had been looking at the garden steadily since the previous evening, when her husband had told her they were moving to Atsugi. She tried to remember what life had been like for her before the garden was built. The least that could be said was that, then, she had been innocent. Since the garden was completed, however, she had not known where she had come from or where she was going. From the day she had learned that Kase was the one who had come to build the garden, until today—she went over the whole period in her mind. She felt she had been walking though a withered field all along. Her mind went back to when she was eighteen years old, to that autumn evening when she returned home to find Old Kane working in the garden with a young man. She had seen his profile and it had had a certain rigidity about it that made him seem distant and unapproachable. Something of that character still remained in Kase today. She wondered if it would always be there. How could she possibly get through her remaining years if this man turned his back on her? But even if she did leave her family, she would not necessarily be the sole object of Kase's love. She recalled the road that led to her family-'s graves, a road buried deep in last year's fallen leaves. What if she sought death? Could that have been what drove her to Kase?

The long shadows of the trees disappeared and the garden lost its depth. Everything seemed level and flat just before evening closed in. Already the overwhelming darkness of the night was enfolding her.